FAKE IT FOR ME

A Secret Baby Romance

R. S. ELLIOT

Cover Design by Cover Couture

www.bookcovercouture.com

❀ Created with Vellum

GET YOUR FREE BOOK

Have you read the FREE Prequel to Beauty and the BOSS?

If not, sign up for my Newsletter and download your FREE book.

Click this Link to Download your FREE book

Beauty and the BOSS is the first book in the Billionaire's Obsession Series and is available here -> Read Beauty and the BOSS

Lawyer and the BOSS is the 2nd book in the Billionaire's Obsession Series and is available here -> Read Lawyer and the BOSS

Nanny and the BOSS is the 3rd book in the Billionaire's Obsession Series and is available here -> Read Nanny and the BOSS

Teacher and the BOSS is the 4th book in the Billionaire's Obsession Series and is available here -> Read Teacher and the BOSS

Innkeeper and the BOSS is the 5th and final book in the Billionaire's Obsession Series and is available here -> Read Innkeeper and the BOSS

FORBIDDEN FAIRY TALES

I am so excited to introduce my new series "***Forbidden Fairy Tales***". Each book in this series is a standalone and can be read in any order.

Forbidden Professor is Book 1 in this series and is the story of Aly and Zach.

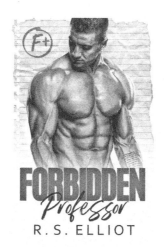

Click this link to read Forbidden Professor

Forbidden Firefighter is Book 2 in this series and is the story of Lyndsey and Hunter.

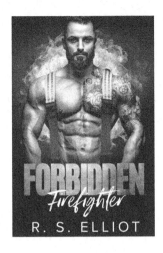

Click this link to read Forbidden Firefighter

My Forbidden Boss is Book 3 in this series and is the story of Stella and Adam.

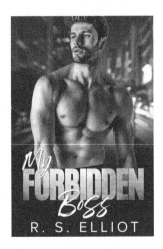

Click this Link to read My Forbidden Boss

Forbidden Doctor is Book 4 in this series and is the story of Stevie and Adrian.

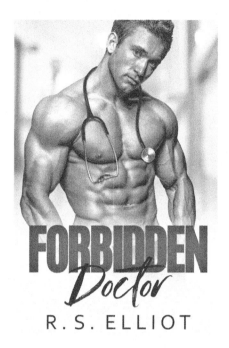

Click this Link to read Forbidden Doctor

Chapter One

JUSTIN

"*J*ust handle it."

I'd had enough of this lecture. It was always the same issue. Always the same requirements.

"Handle it?" Kinsley shouted, her pale blue eyes closing into thin little slats of rage. Her lips puckered as she inhaled one sharp draw of breath to soothe the rising tempest. It was about par for the course in our relationship. The woman was three years younger than me, but she acted more like a big sister than anything else. "This is your assistant we're talking about. You need to be the one doing the interview."

I shrugged and exhaled my own sigh of exasperation. "I mean, fuck! How difficult can it be, Kinsley? Does the girl know how to get coffee? Can she type? There really isn't much to it. Can't we just get a robot to do the job?"

"Can she manage clients with ease and grace?" Kinsley added. "Is she personable? She's the first person your clients are going to meet before dealing with you. She needs to be a reflection of the company, someone who can make good judgment calls without you at times."

Good God, I don't have time for all of this! I was thirty minutes away from missing my flight to Arizona. If I missed that flight, there went my meeting with an investment worth millions of dollars and a hotel acquisition I'd spent upwards of three months trying to win.

"Then, I leave that to your judgment, darling. I've got a plane to catch," I said, and turned down the hallway toward the exit.

Three months was already outside of my typical closing range. I usually made deals within a matter of minutes, solidified mergers within hours. Though lately, it felt like I was losing my touch. What the hell was happening to me? Was this what it was like to get old? Not only was the Arizona deal taking an excruciating amount of time, but the Montgomery Plantation in Louisiana had been a thorn in my side since May.

Fucking May! Five months—almost six now—and the plantation owner still hadn't agreed to meet me. Not to mention, I'd drawn up a pretty fantastic offer no one should refuse.

But she had. And that was enough to piss me off for five straight months. No wonder I'd gone through six assistants in such a short amount of time.

"She needs to know what she's getting into with your arrogant ass," Kinsley shouted down the hallway at me.

Who was she talking about now? The plantation owner? My assistant? God knows my assistant didn't need to be a woman. I'd made men quit just as fast as the women, but I refused to accept any less than the best. I demanded results from every member of my staff. If they couldn't provide that, they weren't worth my time.

"Is that any way to speak to the head of the company?" I asked, smugly, turning back to face her.

Kinsley pointed to the sign plastered over the door frame on the wall, the one that read: "Alexander & Dawson Holdings."

"You forget that's my name up there, too, asshole," she snapped. "And you're not exactly the most personable of people yourself."

My shoulders sagged forward. "Is this about Darlene?"

"Of course, it's about Darlene!" Kinsley shouted. "The woman cried almost every day on her lunch break before finally snapping and trying to kill you."

To be fair, it was with a letter opener, and the woman was somewhere in the range of four feet ten and five feet even. There wasn't much damage she could have done to a six feet two man with such a mediocre weapon, even if I wasn't built like a brick and didn't have military training. It was actually quite pathetic seeing her dangling from the wrists, the office supply still in hand, and her little feet flailing about like a toddler trying to escape bathtime. I had opted out of pressing charges, but apparently, the State had rules about those kinds of things.

"Some people just can't handle the pressure," I said finally.

"Pressure my ass. You need to set boundaries as a boss. You expect someone to be on your beck and call, day and night."

"I pay them a generous salary to be on my beck and call." It wasn't like they were getting paid in peanuts. I paid almost twice the industry rate for an assistant, plus benefits. With that kind of cash, they should be happy to have a job as easy as this one. A few extra hours, a little frustration, it was all worth it for the salary they were making. Hell, did no one value hard work anymore? They expected everything to come easy and with as much reward as possible.

Life didn't work that way. It certainly hadn't for me.

"They need time to sleep and refresh to even be available to you the following day," Kinsley explained. "Your expectations are too high."

I waved off her concerns with a dismissive hand. "Then we will try again with this next person."

"We could hire *two* people."

"That's too confusing."

Kinsley tossed up her hands and emitted something that sounded like a curse under her breath. "Then you at least need to be kinder to this one."

"I was kind to Darlene." *Sort of.*

"You told her she didn't know how to make coffee," Kinsley said, placing her hands on her hips and tilting her head to the side in her usual, patronizing manner.

Even with the obvious disgust in her gaze pinning me where I stood, I failed to see what was so wrong with my comment. "She didn't."

"She bought it at the coffee shop."

I shrugged. "A mix-up of words. I meant she couldn't order it."

"It was your *exact* order." Her voice raised another octave higher. "The same one you order every day. You just didn't want it."

"Well, she should be able to anticipate that."

"Anticipate when you want to change your usual coffee order?" Kinsley's brows dipped to a tiny little *v* in the corner of her forehead. She looked damn near ready to slap me if I moved an inch closer.

I was not accustomed to backing down when anyone confronted me. Hell, I wasn't even used to being talked to like this at all. Most knew better and were rightfully too afraid to question my judgment. The others simply went along with whatever I said hoping to get something better in return. My hotheaded business partner was quite possibly the only person left on the planet who could get away with berating me like I was five. She was certainly the only one who even attempted it.

It didn't make anything she said any easier.

"A good assistant will know how to soothe me when I'm upset," I explained. "Put that down in your notes for the interview."

"'Soothe you' when you're upset? What are you, two? Justin, it wasn't just the coffee. You made her feel like she couldn't do anything right."

That wasn't entirely off. The woman was hopeless. I was doing her a service really by letting her stay employed at all.

"We can't keep replacing an assistant every couple of weeks just so you can berate them. Darlene lasted the longest, and we both know how that ended."

"I can handle an attempt on my life or two."

"I don't want you to handle an attempt on your life." Kinsley reached out and thumped my shoulder. "I want you to be a decent human being for once and treat these people with respect. Otherwise, I'm going to be the one to kill you."

Her blue eyes glossed over with a glare as cold as ice, and she swiftly closed the distance between us in a few short steps. "And we both know I'll succeed."

I groaned, casting a glance at my phone to check the time. Fuck. I needed all of this to be over. It was too early for me to be dealing with these lectures. "Fine. I'll back off. But I'm leaving you to find me the right fit. None of this just trying to find a body to fill the space. He or she needs to be worth their salt."

"And the Montgomery Plantation?" she asked, halting me in my tracks yet again. Damn. The woman always knew how to get to me. "How do you plan on handling that?"

"That's my business, not yours," I said over my shoulder. "So, don't worry about it."

"Seems to me we're partners in this business. That means equal sharing and all that."

I grit my teeth. "Don't worry about it."

"I have to worry about it. It's the whole reason you're even acting like a dick in the first place."

"Damn it, Kinsley. I said I'll handle it. Now just leave it alone."

Her cool stare assessed me like a lion sizing up a small elephant, contemplating whether she and all her defenses could take me down if necessary. "Fine. But what's so special about Louisiana anyway?"

I grumbled. "Nothing."

"Wait. Isn't that where—"

"I said, it's nothing. So it is. Nothing." I had to go. All this nonsense was getting me nowhere. I didn't get where I was by worrying about other people's feelings. My first million didn't magically fall into my bank account or come from me questioning myself and my motivations.

I worked my ass off. I made the tough calls whenever needed, and I got the job done.

Only this acquisition was different. It wasn't for the company. Not exactly. This meant more to me than all of my millions, and it was the one thing in my entire career that wasn't going according to plan.

"Right," Kinsley said, tugging me free from my memories. "Because your recent behavior has nothing to do with your inability to land a deal in your home state."

I opened my mouth to argue, but she cut me off. "Look, I don't know how close this property comes to home, but you've got to stop beating yourself up about what happened to Peter."

My jaw clicked. "We're done here."

I pivoted on my heel and headed toward the door. *Not today. Hell, no.*

"Fine, but you're on a tight leash when you get back," Kinsley called down the hallway after me. "Best behavior, you hear me?"

Best behavior? Yeah, right.

Chapter Two

ELIZA

"Why do you want to work here?" Kinsley Dawson asked.

The Kinsley Dawson of Alexander and Dawson Holdings.

I was so starstruck by the woman standing in front of me I could barely even answer the question. All I could do was sit there, staring blankly while she patiently awaited my response.

Who could blame me? The woman was a total badass. Working her way up the corporate ladder from practically nothing, busting through that glass ceiling like some warrior queen laying down the groundwork for every other woman who followed, Kinsley Dawson was a legend. And in case all of that wasn't enough to totally intimidate and awe anyone who encountered her, she was also a former marine.

She and her partner, Justin Alexander, had formed their hotel company just a little over seven years ago and quickly grew to become one of the most notable chains in the country.

And while I sat there fangirling over a woman who might

very well dismiss me at any moment, I completely forgot the question she'd even asked. I was already off to a great start.

"Could you repeat the question?" I asked.

"Why do you want to work here?" Kinsley repeated, showing no visible signs of irritation. Either she was used to people gawking at her like some celebrity, or she was a phenomenal poker player.

I must have rehearsed the answer to that question a thousand times because I want to spearhead my career in the hotel industry. I also want to put this otherwise useless information I received from a partially completed hospitality degree to use.

Also, I need the money. Bad.

I must have sent out my resume to hundreds of potential employers. Each one of them would have placed me well within reach of my dreams, whether it got me there in two years or ten. This was the only one to respond.

It was the only one worth my time, really. I already had a part-time job at DSW working the typical nights and weekends. The pay was adequate but not enough to take care of my parents. And my family could use all the help they could get.

We all could.

This job promised a generous salary, but that wasn't the only appealing thing to working here. Not only did it place me among corporate gods like Kinsley Dawson and Justin Alexander, it put me in the path of working with some of the top companies all across the market. I would learn my way around the world of hospitality and tourism, network with some of the most powerful investors in the company, and eventually accrue either enough money to go back to school or enough experience to merit a career on my own.

"I went to school for hospitality," I explained. "So, I am ready to pursue a career that will allow me to use that degree."

"Did you graduate?"

Ugh. We were already off to a horrible start.

I shook my head. "No."

"Why not?"

How did I answer that? If I told her the real reason, she might see a sympathetic side to me. Something that didn't scream lazy or unfocused. Something that instead sounded dedicated and loyal.

Or would it be oversharing? Would it seem like a weakness? Maybe she'd worry I wouldn't show up when needed, or that I might have to drop everything in the event of an emergency.

Because I would.

I wouldn't want to work for a company that didn't understand my situation. I needed the money, but family always came first.

"My dad was diagnosed with cancer a year ago," I said. "My mom needed help with doctor's appointments, the house, and the bills. So, I took time off from school to help."

Ms. Dawson's eyes softened, appraising me either with pity or respect. I was too nervous to distinguish between the two. "Are you able to work forty hours a week?"

"Absolutely."

"What about more?"

"I am not averse to hard work," I said. "Or a full schedule. I can do the hours required, within reason."

Ms. Dawson's lip quirked upward as if something in my final stipulation amused her. "And do you know what your limitations are? I mean, do you know when too much is too much? How not to overload yourself with more work than you can handle? Are you organized?"

I inhaled a steadying draw of breath. How was I supposed to answer something like that? It was a rapid-fire round of questions, and I wasn't entirely sure what she meant by any of them. Was she expecting me to make my own schedule, to communicate when enough was enough? I suppose it wasn't completely unheard of. They wanted to ensure I would say "no" and not leave them high and dry when someone else with more time could complete the task.

But the job was for an assistant. Not even to Ms. Dawson but to her partner. How much freedom with my schedule would I be given, especially when the job was meant to be a nine to five?

"I know my limits, yes," I said carefully, suspicious as to where these answers lead me.

She tapped her pen against the notepaper in front of her, glancing up at me through the mischievous tilt of her gaze. A smile curved one corner of her lips. "How good are you at dealing with difficult people?"

It seemed like an innocent enough question. It definitely wasn't my first time being asked it. After all, I'd worked in retail. Every employer expected you to know how to deal with difficult clients and diffuse a potentially tumultuous situation before it festered out of hand.

Still ...

Something in the curve of Ms. Dawson's mouth and the glimmer of humor in her pale eyes sparked an instinct of caution within me. What in the hell was I getting myself into?

"Dealing with difficult people is a way of life now, isn't it?" I shrugged. "I like to think of it as handling a challenging situation, rather than an unreasonable person. The outbursts and anger of an individual are usually no more than the product of a deeper-seated, underlying issue. Maybe they had a bad day or a bad experience in the past. Getting to the root of that problem is part of helping the client achieve an optimum experience."

"And if there is no underlying issue? What if the client is genuinely just a horrible person?"

Good God. What was this woman trying to tell me? All these subliminal hints were doing nothing for my resolve.

I need the money. I need the experience. I can handle an ornery client or two.

"I don't believe there are any truly horrible people." I heard myself say the words, though I didn't entirely believe they'd come from my mouth. Did I just say something so idealistic that I might as well be puking sunshine and gliding on rainbows?

Even Ms. Dawson reacted with a mix of surprise and disgust. She tipped her head back, narrowing her eyes as if assessing how sincere my answer was.

Was it sincere? Did I really think there were no bad people in the world? That wasn't exactly what I said, though it might as well have been. I wasn't so foolish to believe the world was a star-filled wonderland where nothing bad ever happened. The market was flooded with entitled people, with those who thought themselves above others without any reason or thought. These are careless, devious creatures who tore each other down just to make themselves feel better, and who would never see reason, no matter how hard I tried.

And yet ...

Everyone deserved a chance to prove themselves. Didn't they?

"Well, Miss Cortez," Kinsley Dawson drawled out my name with the same questionable smile from before. "I would love the chance to prove you wrong."

She reached her hand across the table, and I accepted it hesitantly.

"Welcome to the team," she added. "You start tomorrow."

I'd been given very clear instructions about what to pick up in the morning.

Apparently, my new boss was arriving back from a late flight, and the first thing he would want in the morning was his coffee. A tall blonde with one cream and no sugar. Probably the same way he liked his women.

Didn't all billionaires want a tall blonde?

I arrived in the lobby of the massive building and approached the reception area in the center. The woman behind the counter snickered as she checked me in and handed me my badge. I'd taken the photo the day before, right after Ms. Dawson had offered me the job. I'd filled out all the necessary paperwork and was given a tour of my new workplace. I already knew where my desk was located, just outside my boss's door as I had seen in all those movies about fresh-faced interns ready to brave the unknown.

It was all becoming too real, too fast. This step might determine the next phase of my life and put me on the path toward what I really wanted: to see the world. Travel was a luxury our family never really could afford. The daughter of first-generation immigrants from Peru, I had everything I could ever need, though we were by no means rich. I became obsessed with the tourism industry at a young age, particularly hotels and their many different aesthetic qualities and amenities. There were hotels carved into the sides of mountains, those built within the walls of an ancient castle, and others embedded beneath a blanket of stars and the Northern Lights in an untouched wilderness.

I wanted to see them all. I wanted to help others enjoy them and find all the comfort I did reading about them as a child. This job would take me there. It would show me how to run a company as amazing as this one under the guidance of two powerhouses like Alexander and Dawson.

A rush of people emptied out of the elevator ahead of me. I pressed myself up against the wall to let them pass. The coffee cups in my hands teetered precariously in their holster as each onlooker brushed past me without a glance in my direction.

I never felt so invisible.

I'd offered to bring Ms. Dawson her special blend as well, since carting three cups of coffee hadn't seemed like a challenge at the time. Only now, trying to keep the cups in the flimsy little carrying case the barista supplied me with while dodging cell phone addicted suits, seemed like a trial straight out of Greek tragedy.

I attempted to navigate through the crowd, swerving out of the way as best I could to avoid the traffic. The barrage of people cleared just a few more feet ahead. If I could make it just a little bit further ...

The carton tumbled out of my hands. I slammed into something as hard as a rock, while a soft burn slowly rippled up my arms.

"Fuck!" Someone shouted. "Holy Mother of God."

The man had appeared out of nowhere with his head buried in his phone, leaving me only seconds to react to weave around him. Which I hadn't. Instead, he slammed right into me sending the carton of coffee cups crashing against his chest and splattering the both of us in scalding hot coffee.

The initial shock stole away from the searing pain in my body, forcing me to tend to the man I'd unintentionally burned.

"I'm so sorry," I said, frantically dabbing at the brown stain on his chest with the sleeve of my sweater. "Are you okay?"

"No, I'm not okay," he snapped, and yanked my hands away. "You just poured hot coffee all over me."

I reeled backward, staring up at the man in front of me with caution. He was tall and well-built, an intimidating specimen who could frighten the hell out of any normal person without the added bonus of him yelling at them. But I was no normal person, and this man was in no way faultless in this little escapade.

"To be fair, I didn't 'pour' it all over you," I corrected. "You ran into me and it spilled."

His bright gray eyes collided with mine, turning as dark as storm clouds rolling across a clear sky. "Oh, so this is my fault?"

I nudged my chin a notch higher, refusing to be bullied by a man who clearly thought himself so high above me. "You were the one staring down at your phone instead of watching where you were going."

"And you were obviously paying enough attention for the both of us," he said, removing a handkerchief from his pocket to scrub the coffee from his pants. "Why didn't you just move out of my way?"

What? Oh no, he didn't. This man just told me I should have been watching for him?

The hell I should have.

How was I even supposed to respond to something like that? The man quite clearly saw nothing wrong with his actions. There could be no reasoning with someone like that.

"Is that how it works?" I asked, instead. "You just do as you please, and everyone just works around you?"

He set his jaw, once again pinning me with his stony glare. "You're lucky I don't sue you or have you arrested for assault."

"Assault?" Oh, this man was trying my patience. If I was going down for assault, I was going to make sure it counted. "Are you insane? It was an accident. Anyone with a brain could see that."

"No, someone with a brain could obviously move out of a person's way fast enough."

My mouth dropped open. "I couldn't move from where I was standing. You were walking too fast. Not that I need to justify my actions to an arrogant son of a ..."

Do not start a fight on your first day of work. Do not start a fight on your first day of work.

I had never been in a fight in my life. Hell, I'd never been in any sort of public altercation like this. I wanted to see the best in people. I really did. But this man was impossible.

"You know what?" I narrowed my eyes over him. "I'm glad I spilled coffee all over your suit."

He feigned a horrified gasp. "Well, fuck. How am I ever going to come back from an insult like that?"

"You are an insufferable excuse for a man," I said, only slightly thrown off when his lips curled at the end. Almost as if he was enjoying how worked up I was getting. "It was an accident, not something done out of clumsiness or maliciousness. I didn't expect an apology on your part, but I did expect a little understanding."

Nothing. The grin at his mouth slowly drooped into something serious and partly sinister, as if I'd finally hit a nerve that resonated with him.

Good!

"Now, if you'll excuse me," I said. "I need to go find someone to help me clean this up."

I brushed past him and found my way to the nearest custodian. My hands trembled as I pointed out the location of the spill, my heart still thundering like the hoofbeats of a thousand wild horses in my ears. Even the custodian took pity on me and told me to go clean myself up.

Perfect! My first day of work and I'd almost come close to murdering another co-worker in the building. I had no coffee to deliver to either of my bosses, I was twenty minutes late, and I looked a complete mess with my clothes covered in coffee stains.

If this was a sign of things to come, maybe I wasn't cut out for any of this. I made myself as presentable as possible and hurried up the elevator to the top floor. Ms. Dawson greeted me as soon as I got off the elevator.

"Where the hell have you been?" she asked, barely looking at me. It was a small consolation; she might not even notice my horrific attire. "He's in rare form at the moment. I'm sorry. You're going to need to figure out what's wrong with him."

Ms. Dawson knocked on the door to his office. A curt

"enter" grumbled past the barricade of wood, and within seconds, she hurtled me inside.

The door slammed behind me.

The man behind the desk straightened, his cold, gray eyes drinking in the sight of me with a blend of amusement and frustration.

No, no, no! There is no way my luck could be this terrible!

"Ah. It's you," he said, tersely. "Guess, I don't need to ask where my coffee is."

Chapter Three

JUSTIN

"This isn't going to work out," I said.

There was no way this woman would ever suit as my assistant. She couldn't even handle something as simple as a coffee run, let alone manage any situation with grace and charm.

She shook her head, my words slowly sinking in. "What?"

"I need someone who can do their job, and quite frankly, I don't think that's you."

"You have no idea what I'm capable of yet," she said.

I scoffed and set my focus on sorting out the papers on my desk. All things she would have been handling if that little coffee incident downstairs hadn't been enough to reveal her true colors. The last thing I wanted was someone who couldn't control their temper.

"I already know that fetching a few cups of coffee is beyond your realm of abilities," I explained. "So, I shudder to think what you would do with more complicated tasks."

She only blinked, peering back at me with eyes the color of sunshine and whiskey. "You're serious?"

"Absolutely."

"You're firing me?" The space between us dissolved in a matter of two quick steps. She neared the edge of my desk, the final obstacle dividing us. A flash of memories surrounding letter openers and disgruntled assistants pulsed through my mind. "It hasn't even been an hour yet."

"No, it's been a half hour. And you were late."

"Because I was picking up a mess *you* helped me make."

Yet another reason this would never work. No one talked to me like that. Ever. Certainly not some lowly assistant who needed me to pay her bills. People feared me, respected me. They did not scold me like a parent catching her teenager jumping curfew.

The only person who ever got away with it was ...

Kinsley.

I grit my teeth. Damn the woman. Was this some sort of retribution for sticking her with the interview? Was she somehow making me atone for my sins with an assistant as stubborn and thoughtless as this one? There was no other explanation. How in hell had this woman passed the interview process unless Kinsley saw her employment as some grand joke at my expense?

"So, not only do you refuse to apologize to your boss about covering him in scalding hot coffee," I said. "you are actually blaming me for the entire incident?"

"I did apologize, but you didn't want to hear it." She was holding back, steadying herself with a calming breath to prevent jumping down my throat.

Maybe I needed to ease off. Maybe I was letting all this frustration with the Montgomery Plantation manifest into unnecessary anger. I was lashing out at everyone: Kinsely, Darlene ... whoever this woman was. I hadn't even glanced at her file yet, and already I wanted her gone.

"And I didn't say it was *all* your fault," she added. "I admitted my role in this mess, even if I couldn't move out of the way fast enough."

Fuck ... she sounded sincere. We'd both had a rough start, and I sure as hell wasn't making a good first impression. I was being a dick. I could admit it. Not to her, of course, but at least to myself.

Everything I wanted, I got one way or another, though it never took this long. Five months, five freaking months of hell had made me this way. Why didn't Rosalie Montgomery just forfeit the plantation already? Put all of us out of our misery? I wasn't anywhere close to relenting. I'd wear her down eventually.

Though, all the while, I was the one being worn down.

What's so special about Louisiana anyway?

There was nothing special about it. Not to me. Or so I told myself. It was the only way to right a wrong ten years in the making. The only way to ignore the ghosts haunting my every nightmare.

Kinsley had begged me to play nice. Hell, she'd demanded it. I couldn't afford to go another day without an assistant, not with my life falling to pieces in the wake of the Montgomery family's reluctance. So, I was stuck with this one, a woman whose name I still had not bothered to learn.

I could do worse.

My eyes captured hers in a silent challenge. She met me head on, bold, and unyielding—everything I hated in a subordinate.

And yet, something about her reminded me of that strong-willed, idealistic person from my youth. A glint of hope shimmered in her golden gaze, like streaks of sunlight cresting over the horizon. She wanted to see the good in me, to believe I wouldn't cast her out on the turn of a dime if it suited me, that there was a little good left in me, after all.

I leaned forward, planting my hands on top of my desk and tilting down to her level. Her plump lips parted as I closed the last bit of distance between us, and I tried my damndest not to notice them. Though, the more time I spent with this woman, the more increasingly aware I became of how distracting she might be.

"What's your name?" I asked suddenly, my voice a low grumble. Damn it! What the hell was wrong with me?

"Eliza Cortez," she said.

A smirk curled at my lips, and she tilted her chin upward in defiance. The motion drew my attention down to her mouth, the deep shade of red lipstick she wore, and thoughts about how her lips might feel wrapped around my cock. As if summoned, the gentle tug of my erection coming to life acted more as a warning than anything else.

Two minutes ago, I was ready to fire this woman and toss her out without another thought. Now, I was allowing myself to engage in fantasies better left unexplored. I really was losing my mind.

"Fine." My eyes flicked upward, finding hers once again. "You want another chance. I'll give it to you, but it won't come easy."

I leaned back off the desk and made my way to a tall cabinet on the other side of the room. First things first, my shirt had to go.

I shrugged off the suit jacket and tossed it over the side of a nearby chair. Heat permeated the air like a cloud hovering between us. Whether this arose from the residual effects of the coffee or my wandering thoughts, I couldn't tell. But I needed to put on something less stifling, fast.

"What are you doing?" Eliza asked, all but shouting as I unhooked the top two buttons on my shirt.

"Changing." Amusement tugged at my lips once again at the sound of her apparent confusion. "Don't worry. It isn't that kind of a deal. I have a meeting with a client in fifteen minutes, and I really can't afford to walk in there with coffee stains on my shirt, now can I?"

I quickly freed the remaining buttons and cast the soiled shirt to the ground. Luckily, I kept a spare shirt or two in the cabinet in the event of such accidents occurring. Though, to be fair, this was the first time I'd needed to use it.

"It's a little ... distracting," she said.

The softness in her voice caught me off guard. I faced her, surprised to see her appraising me with almost as much appreciation as I had her mere moments before. Her stare darkened to amber gemstones, running down along the length of my torso as if she might pounce on me at any moment.

Fuck me! How the hell was I to keep my hands to myself when her eyes whispered desires neither one of us was ready to pursue.

"Enjoying the view?" I asked.

Eliza snapped her head to the side. The muscle in her jaw twitched, and she inhaled one long, shaky breath. "Isn't there somewhere private you could do that?"

"Yes. My office. Which I'm currently in," I explained. Where else did she expect me to go? She was the one encroaching on my space, not the other way around. "If you don't like it, you can leave."

She huffed in annoyance and pivoted on her heel toward the door. Though, instead of walking out as I'd expected, she just stood there, facing the opposite direction and ignoring me completely.

"What do you need from me this morning?" she asked.

My mind had already started to wander to other things. Lewd, senseless things driven by my cock alone and nothing else. It was hard not to when I had a fantastic view of the most perfect ass I'd ever seen. My gaze traveled up her hips, tracing her thin waist and the lush curves of her body with a ravenous hunger reserved for men who'd spent years in prison.

Again, my cock rose to attention, trained like the faithful soldier he was to recognize a fine specimen of erotic beauty when he found it. And my God, the woman was gorgeous.

This woman is trouble.

When was the last time I had sex? Clearly, that was the real problem here. A nice, hard fuck was exactly what I needed to get my head back on straight. I would loosen up about the Montgomery place, blow off some steam, and stop fantasizing about an assistant I could hardly stand to be around.

"I need you to research the history of the Montgomery Plantation," I said, slipping into the crisp, clean shirt and setting to work on the buttons. "There should be a file left behind by my last assistant that covers most of the property's information. We've been trying to land the account for months, but the owner isn't budging."

"Did the owner say why?"

"If she had, we would not still be in this predicament," I explained, and finished the last button on my shirt. I grabbed my coat from the chair and walked around the desk toward her.

"Shouldn't we be doing research on the client instead?" Eliza asked.

I leaned into her ear, somehow empowered by the slight start she gave at the sound of my voice. "It's all in the file, sweetheart."

Her eyes narrowed as I moved in front of her and shoved my hands into my pockets. She was actually kind of adorable when angry—like a rabid kitten.

"You need to read it over," I said, sensing an objection or argument brewing somewhere within the dark confines of her thoughts. "Memorize it and commit every last detail to memory within the next couple of days."

"Very well." She nodded. One hand nervously stroked her forearm, drawing my attention to the bright red mark near her wrist.

Instinctively, I reached out and gripped her hand between my fingers. I tilted her wrist upward, exposing the red splotch of skin to my examination. "What happened?"

She scoffed. "It's nothing."

The pad of my thumb stroked over the sensitive area, and she winced despite all pretenses. I really was an ass. I'd been so concerned about my shirt and my pride, I hadn't even thought about whether she'd been harmed in any way by our collision.

"You need to put something cool on it," I said. "There should be an ice pack in the fridge in the breakroom that you can wrap in a cloth. Otherwise, Ms. Dawson might have some aloe vera in her office. She has a whole medical supply chest in there."

Eliza nodded, her gaze focused intently on me and the hands still holding her. I hadn't forgotten to let go. I just didn't want to.

Trouble.

I released her. Both hands dove back into my pockets, where they belonged. They certainly weren't meant to be anywhere near my new assistant's body. No matter how badly I wanted them there.

"Anything else?" she asked, trembling either with need or shock that I'd touched her at all. It was too soon to tell which.

I shook my head and moved toward the door. "Since I didn't get my coffee this morning, I'll expect something caffeinated when I get back. Just nothing hot this time."

Chapter Four

ELIZA

"It's been five days and Gabi ..." I inhaled one long stiff breath to keep from screaming. "I want to kill him."

"That seems a little extreme," she said, checking the sizes on the pair of shoes in front of her before placing them up on the shelf.

"*He's* a little extreme," I explained, joining her for our nightly ritual of organizing the shelves. Or at least it's our ritual on the nights we worked together at the shoe store. "I can't do anything right. It's either the coffee is too cold, or I didn't add enough toner to the copier machine, or I missed one comma in a 4,000 page proposal form."

I slammed a box of stilettos onto the shelf, sending the entire fixture rattling in warning. Both Gabi and I immediately threw our hands out to brace for the repercussions: tumbling sandals and slingbacks, a drooping shelf, or the entire unit collapsing on us. From the force with which I'd knocked into it, one would have thought something would happen.

Nothing did. Thankfully. I couldn't afford to replace an industrial shelving unit, let alone find another job now that I'd taken on this new nightmare position under Mr. Alexander. Sure, it paid enough to cover most of the bills, but I still needed help. I still planned on going back to school, and right now, I needed both jobs to save up for that.

"Sorry," I said sheepishly, receiving a disappointed glare no woman should ever have to receive from her baby sister. "But he just makes me so mad. I just finished out my first week of the job. Doesn't that give me at least a little bit of leniency in terms of perfectionism?"

"I don't know. Some jobs are just like that."

"I guess."

Gabi pivoted at the waist, cocking her hip to the side and raising up a finger as if struck with an epiphany. "I had a professor who refused to give any of his students an *A*. He said there was no such thing as a perfect paper. It's not a bad thing. Some people just always look for areas of improvement."

Somehow that didn't make me feel any better. Yes, moving forward and constantly improving was important, but so was morale. Knowing you're not a complete failure at life, or having even some semblance of job security, was something I desperately needed to help me feel sane at the moment. I felt as though I might lose my job at any moment with him.

"If you need validation in your workplace, then that's something that you just might have to note for your career in the future," Gabi said. "Or you might need to find somewhere else to get it entirely."

"It's not only that." *God, I don't want to have this conversation anymore.*

I hated complaining. I always wanted to look on the positive side of things and strive to keep others hopeful and motivated despite the hardships. But it was virtually hopeless with a man like Justin Alexander. And when my sister had asked me how my day was going five days into my journey through Hell, I couldn't stop myself from blurting out my problems. "It's the nonstop demands. He calls me at all hours of the night, Gabi."

My sister's eyes lit up like Christmas trees at a lighting ceremony. "Do you mean like a booty call?"

"No." The word flew out like a scoff more than a denial. I couldn't have sounded more horrified if I tried. The mere thought of Mr. Alexander calling me for such things was completely unthinkable. And yet, I couldn't get the image of his half naked body out of my mind. Who knew a man could even be built like that? All this time, I thought only movie stars or athletes or guys with way too much time on their hands could look the way he did.

Oh my God. No!

All these thoughts were dangerous. Not only was I completely inexperienced when it came to men, he was my boss. A cantankerous asshole, for lack of a better word, who would crush my soul and then dance on the fiery ashes of my heart without a second thought.

"Is he cute?" Gabi asked, reading the film reel of emotions playing out across my face as I tried to devise any other topic of conversation.

Heat climbed up my throat, choking me with its cloying fingers. "He's ok, I guess."

Who was I kidding? *The boy was fine as hell!*

"Uh huh, right. So that dazed look on your face a few

minutes ago had nothing to do with him taking his shirt off in front of you the other day?"

"Stop!" Ugh. Why was this happening? Wasn't it bad enough to be working for this man and all of his egotistical standards without imagining what the rest of him might look like naked? I'd already had to talk myself out of ridiculous daydreams of him throwing me on top of his desk and giving me very explicit orders about what he wanted.

It went against every fiber of my being. I was the one who liked being in control. I liked having everything organized and orchestrated down to the millisecond. But as a twenty-three-year-old virgin with absolutely no experience charming the opposite sex, I was marginally aware of the need for guidance in the one area I knew nothing about.

"You're doing it again," Gabi said.

"Doing what?" I shook my head and set to work down the next row of shoes.

"Staring off into space with a look that is definitely not customer appropriate."

I released a mangled breath that was somewhere between a sigh and a growl. "I don't know what you're talking about. He calls incessantly about things he needs for the following morning, or he sends me reminders to go over materials for a company. He is a demanding, self-absorbed cretin who can't seem to get his shit together on his own."

"Hmm." Gabi cocked her head to the side, a disbelieving smirk on her face. "Do people our age use the word 'cretin'?"

"It just isn't anything that I thought it was going to be," I explained. "I imagined myself being able to network, to learn more about how the company runs itself, and how to interact with clients. But instead, I'm fetching coffee and making sure that he has all of his dates in order."

"Well, that's part of running a company, too. It's just not the parts that you're interested in doing at the moment," Gabi said, coming in all too true as the voice of reason. "You want to jump into the waters like this is your summer vacation in Tahiti. It doesn't work like that. These aren't warm, inviting currents ready to wrap you up and let you coast into the next phase of your life. This is the Polar Bear Swim. You need to work your ass off before you can even dip a toe in the water."

Was there anything more annoying than receiving a lecture from your little sister? I was supposed to be the responsible one, the one who everyone leaned on and looked to for guidance. But instead, Gabi was the one lecturing me about sucking it up and dealing with my decisions like a grown-up.

"Fine. I can work my ass off," I said. "That's not a problem. But I feel like I need to breathe. How am I supposed to work here, take care of Mama and Papi, and meet my boss's demands on a twenty-four hour basis? Not to mention find time to sleep."

"Come on. It isn't that bad."

My fingers dove into my pocket, removing the cellphone that had been vibrating almost nonstop for the past two hours. "He's literally called me three times since I've started this shift. We're two hours in .... and he's calling me again."

The face of the phone lit up in my hands as an irritating little reminder of the fate I'd chosen. There it was, his name and number flashing like a beacon I couldn't ignore.

"Ooh. Really?" Gabi's eyes flashed with intrigue. "You gonna answer it? Let me answer it. I'll talk to him."

"No. Gabi, stop." I jerked the phone away from her. Who

knows how he'd respond if someone else answered, even if it was on accident? Did I even want to answer it now? I was at work. How many times could I duck into the bathroom to take his calls before someone finally realized what was going on? "I can't do this."

Gabi's smile faded and she reached forward to stroke my back. "Hey, it's fine. Just turn it off and put it away."

"I need this job."

"Look, mom and dad will be fine. I can come by this weekend and take over for you. Give you a little break."

A break did sound nice. I worked five days a week at the office, then most evenings at the shoe store along with one weekend day. On days I had off, my mother worked, so it was up to me to keep an eye on our father, make meals for the week, and prepare his medications. These are all the things mom needed help with now that dad had gotten sick.

"Don't you have like a massive final due?" I asked.

"Yeah. But it's like, whatever. I just need to pass."

"Gabi ..."

"It's fine." She groaned. "I can take some time away from my studies to help you. You don't have to do all of this on your own, you know?"

I shook my head. At least the phone stopped ringing anyway. "I thought with this job I'd at least be able to put a little bit of money aside to go back to school."

"Well, I could move back in."

"No. It's fine." We'd had this conversation too many times before. "You're at the house often enough as it is."

"Well, what if I picked up more hours here? Or got a second

part-time job?" Gabi said, jabbing me playfully in the arm. "I could be the assistant to the assistant at your new place."

"Very funny." The last thing I wanted was for my sister to follow in my footsteps. She needed to focus on school, not multiple jobs and the well-being of our parents. That was why I'd even quit school in the first place. I was the older sibling. This was my responsibility. What was the point if both of us were miserable?

"You're doing enough. I just need to set some boundaries at work." That would work, right? If I told Mr. Alexander I was available to work longer hours, rather than this haphazard, disorganized chaos of a schedule he clung to, clearly he would see how much more efficient that would be for the both of us. Wouldn't he?

There was only one way to find out.

Though I was already hating my plan before I'd even set it in motion.

Chapter Five

ELIZA

"This isn't working," I said, staring down Mr. Alexander from where he sat at his desk.

"I couldn't agree more." The smug grin at his lips made me want to reach across and smack him.

I need this job. I need this job.

This man's an idiot.

But I need this job.

"No." I grit my teeth. "You can't keep calling me at all hours of the night. I need some time to sleep, to take care of my own personal things. We need to establish some boundaries."

"Boundaries?" He seemed genuinely shocked, as if no one had ever expressed to him how insane this schedule is. And from the gossip chain around the office, I'd heard that his last assistant had tried to kill him after suffering a mental breakdown. I doubted he was as clueless as he let on. "I didn't think I was crossing too many boundaries. You being my assistant requires you to tend to my needs whenever necessary."

The man was insufferable. "Even you have to admit there is a reasonable limit for something like that. I'm more than happy to spend time outside the forty-hour work week to do whatever you need me to do. However, I need to know my hours ahead of time to have some sort of order to prepare myself."

"That doesn't work for me." He shook his head. "When things come to me, I need you to take note of it."

"No, you need to *take notes*," I corrected. "And then give them to me afterward, in the morning. During regularly scheduled hours."

"But what if it's urgent?"

I tossed my hands into the air. This arguing was getting us nowhere. "It's never urgent. It can always wait until the morning. You just want to be in complete control. I can do my job without being reminded to do something, or look over something, or reread something fifty times a day."

"If you could do your job, you'd be able to handle the hours."

"I have a life outside of this office." The words blurted out like a declaration of war. "I'm sure your girlfriend wouldn't appreciate it if you kept getting phone calls all throughout the night. Let alone that you're the one placing them on a non-stop basis, while also doing work."

Oh my gosh. Did I really just ask him about his girlfriend?

Was I becoming *that* person who casually inquired after someone's relationship status with such a shameless hook? At least I'd thought the illustration held merit before I'd asked it. It was highly unlikely a man who looked like Mr. Alexander and had millions upon millions to burn spent his nights alone, pouring over ledgers and company profiles, and harassing his assistant with phone calls.

Only now that I'd said it, it did sound like I was probing. It wasn't like I hadn't wondered. Especially after our brief moment in his office. The way he'd held my arm and touched me, felt like nothing else I'd ever experienced. Thousands of tiny prickles wove their way up my body at the thought of it. As if on cue, warmth rose to my cheeks, reminding me exactly what I had wanted in that moment. It had nothing to do with revenge, nothing to do with control, and everything to do with giving in to a man who made my blood boil.

"Are you trying to tell me your boyfriend is upset with this arrangement?" he asked, his eyebrow cocked in obvious disgust. "Is that the problem we're facing?"

"I'm saying my life can't be the only one disrupted by this." Or was it? Did he only live for his business? Did he not have any family? No one could tell me anything about the man's personal life, not even Ms. Dawson. All they knew was he never discussed his private life with clients or during press conferences, so they'd assumed he had none of which to speak.

I needed to focus. If this man sensed any hint of weakness, he would not back down. And I needed him to back down; I needed my sanity for God sake! "Having me stay a few extra hours each week is much more efficient for the both of us than stopping everything we're doing every time you have an epiphany."

No response. Only silence and a stony stare across the desk while he leaned into his hand. His cold eyes traveled down the length of me, assessing my willfulness and weighing the odds for how swiftly I might give in. Yet, when his stare rose upward to meet mine, no trace of the same clinical indifference lingered.

Instead, the brewing tempest behind his gaze revealed a hunger that demanded satisfaction.

It fled his expression in an instant. The severe businesslike coldness I was used to returned, leaving me questioning what I even saw.

"So, what is it?" he asked suddenly.

"What is what?" What were we even talking about? This was a ploy, I assumed, men used in any capacity of negotiations. They employed flirtatious gazes to throw a woman off, either making her feel uncomfortable or flattered. That's all this was. It was a tactic to get me to stop arguing.

Or was it?

"Your life outside of this office," he said, standing and moving around to the opposite side of his desk. "The one you so desperately need time away to see to each night."

"I don't see how that—"

"If I need to leave you time to yourself and rearrange my whole way of doing things, then I need to know what your schedule is like." He stopped by one of the oversized chairs facing his desk propping himself against it and standing no more than two feet away from me. "So, what is it? The boyfriend likes his Saturdays open or something?"

Did he just ask me about my boyfriend? Is he assuming I'm doing all of this just to spend time with some man?

You did bring up the whole thing about his girlfriend.

"No. I just ... I have another job."

He shook his head, confused. "I don't pay you enough to just do the one?"

The man seriously had no social skills. It was a wonder he'd managed to run his company as smoothly as he did. Though if our sparring matches were anything to go off of, his negotiation techniques were built on intimidation and manipulation rather than finesse—all things that made me want to wring his neck rather than comply to his demands.

I leveled my gaze over him. "You can't really think that's an appropriate question to ask."

"What I mean is, if I paid you more ..." He rolled his eyes, as if disappointed in himself for even suggesting a pay raise to someone he hated. "... further down the line, obviously, would that make a difference?"

"No. I need ..." What? Time? I needed sanity, though how I articulated that into words he understood had me at a loss. Even if he understood my troubles, it didn't mean he cared. Either way, I just needed to speak my peace then take my next step from there. "I pay most of my parents' bills. My father has been out of work since he started chemo, and my mom went down to part-time to take him to his doctor's appointments and help him around the house."

He stared in silence, assessing the full weight of my situation like a poker player sizing up his opponent. For a moment, a glimpse of something short of sympathy passed within his eyes. His stare darted to the floor, and he adjusted his stance. "I'm sorry to hear that."

Was this sympathy? From the man who'd almost fired me over spilled coffee? I said nothing. It all sounded too much like a trap.

"I'm assuming on the nights and weekends when you are not working either job, you are with your father," he said.

I nodded. "Yes. My mother tries to pick up hours where she can, so I do the cleaning and take care of him. His cancer is ..."

The words caught in my throat. What was wrong with me? Why couldn't I just get through this?

"It's advanced," I said, unable to think of a more delicate way to speak the truth that didn't involve me bursting into tears. "And we can't really afford live-in help at the moment."

"I see."

This is it. This is the part where he fires me for having too many demands at home. My career in hotel management was over before it even began, just like my schooling, just like every other aspect of my life I'd had to put on hold since ...

Since I'd found out my father was sick.

"Fine." He shrugged candidly, taking a step toward me. "We will make it work for now. Send me the hours you're available, and we'll go from there."

"Really?"

The shock in my voice stirred him, and he paused to look at me. "All that arguing and you're surprised you made some semblance of a deal?"

I raised my chin a notch higher. He was standing less than a foot away from me, and I had to crane my neck up to see him clearly. It seriously took away any points of intimidation from me. Not that it mattered. I'd been short my whole life and learned to compensate with a voice no one dared ignore.

"I'm surprised you gave in so easily. That's all," I said, mortified by the trembling in my voice.

What was happening to me? Was he making me nervous? His cold, clipped demeanor I could handle. It was this moderately tender veneer that threw me off, the one that made him seem like he actually cared.

As if he might actually be human.

Plus, he was standing so close to me. God, did he realize how close he was? I could reach out and touch him. What was worse is I wanted to. A thousand urges rose within me to press myself against him, throw my arms around his neck, and imagine myself in one of those wild, wicked fantasies plucked from my fevered dreams.

The same feathery heat crept up my throat, stroking my cheeks with a warning that I was mere seconds away from combusting. He leaned around me, grabbing a piece of paper from the desk behind me. The effects of him being so near made me catch my breath like a cry for help.

He stopped, frozen in place beside me as if afraid he might set off a landmine. His head turned toward me, his lips near my ear.

"Did I frighten you?" His words rumbled in a low growl that tumbled all the way down to the pit of my stomach.

A slim sliver of space still separated us, though I felt every inch of him on my body as if he'd touched me. My chest tightened, slowly strangling what little breath I still possessed. This was the problem with being so good for so long. That had left no time to learn all the sexy things normal women my age did. I was completely lost, out of my element, and hopelessly, thoughtlessly entranced.

"You're just so ..." I struggled for the right words. *Close? Gorgeous? An irresistible temptation to be avoided at all costs?* "Unpredictable."

His eyebrow quirked upward. A grin teetered on the edge of his lips before sinking back into stoic indifference. Except for his eyes. They told an entirely different story.

"You don't like chaos, do you?" He inched forward, slowly

closing the last few inches of distance between us.

I shook my head, partly to answer his question and partly to remind myself of how bad of an idea this was.

He was my boss. A man I despised and had contemplated murdering less than twenty-four hours ago. And if that wasn't enough to repel me, my total lack of experience should have been more than enough to dissuade me. I wouldn't even know what to do if he kissed me. I mean, I knew the basics of it. It wouldn't have been my first attempt, but who knew if I was even any good at it. The last person to kiss me was Jerry Lopez at our senior prom, who'd then dumped me fifteen minutes later for a suite with a blonde and a hot tub.

I'm going to be sick.

Dear, God. No! I may have been inexperienced, but I knew that was the one thing I definitely shouldn't be doing in this situation.

As if compelled by their own desires, my eyes fell to his lips. They couldn't be further than a few inches from me, and yet, I remained frozen in place. No leaning in, no backing away, just standing there waiting for my brain to kick in and finally convince me how wrong all of this was.

"You like to be in control?" he asked.

His gravelled tone surprised me, and I drew my gaze up to meet him. His stare fixated on my mouth in the same hunger I knew must have colored mine. Pressure coiled deep within my stomach, merciless and unforgiving as it sent pulses of pleasure between my legs.

"Yes." My voice was a plea, begging him to take what he wanted despite all the warnings. It terrified me. I wasn't *in* control. I was losing it. Quickly. And not to him but to my own foolish desires. The ones that didn't care that a man like this would ruin me forever. That he would break my heart because I would believe every kiss and every touch was meant for me alone.

I would fall. And he would just pick up and move on to the next acquisition.

"Then tell me what you want," he whispered, a lure drawing me back into the web of temptation. But I had already made up my mind. I needed to end this.

"I ..." I pivoted my head away from him. "I want ... I *need* to get back to my work. You have a meeting with Mrs. Montgomery tomorrow morning, and the papers need proofing. So ..."

He leaned back against one of the armrests on the chair. His arms folded across his chest, and a quizzical stare replaced the intensity there only moments before. To my surprise, he didn't look angry, not even disappointed, just ... concerned. As if he'd misread my feelings and regretted his actions.

But he hadn't misread them.

I'd only allowed myself to indulge in something I shouldn't have and spoiled an already tense relationship for good.

Chapter Six

JUSTIN

"Ineed coffee," I grumbled.

Hell, I needed an aspirin after the night I'd had. If only I could have blamed it on something as heroic as staying up all night doing research, or as epic as a night out drinking. But, no. I spent it tossing and turning and thinking about her.

To be fair, my anxieties about the acquisition had also played a role in my restlessness. We'd waited too long for this interview to let it go up in flames. If Mrs. Montgomery walked out of that door this afternoon without signing the proposal, that deal was as good as gone.

"You have coffee," Kinsley said, directing my attention to the steam cup in my hand.

"I need stronger coffee."

"Have your assistant fetch you some," she said, giggling like some gossiping school girl. "I've heard she's really good at hitting you with the strong stuff."

"What the hell is that supposed to mean?"

Kinsley stopped. Her entire demeanor shifted, one of confusion and caution, as if she needed to ready herself for battle. Maybe she did. The last thing I needed was rumors being spread about me and my goddamn assistant.

"Because … she …" Kinsley struggled for the words, still thrown off by my aggressiveness.

It took me another minute to realize she meant the actual coffee debacle over a week ago and not some lewd, obscure reference. I'd almost forgotten about it. "Oh. The fucking coffee —I don't have time for this. Mrs. Montgomery has finally agreed to this meeting after God knows how long—"

"Six months."

"—And the last thing I need is some half-handed joke about my assistant."

Not to mention, Eliza was the last person I wanted on my mind at that moment. I'd spent half the night imagining what her lips tasted like and whether she would moan in that soft, surrendering way when our mouths met or take command instantly. I imagined my hands cupping that tight, round ass, pulling her body flush against my erection and spreading her wide beneath me. And when I fucked her, she would cry out for me and be completely mine, uncontested.

She would want it—all of it. To surrender all control for once and just give in to pure animalistic ecstasy.

She would want me. But then … she hadn't.

"How is it going by the way?" Kinsley asked.

"What?" I snapped again. Damn, I couldn't even control the outbursts anymore. The woman had me so worked up I either needed to hit something or fuck something. And right now, the odds for me finding relief in either of those areas was not favorable.

"I asked how she was working out," Kinsley explained. "What the heck is wrong with you? You're wound tighter than a top."

"No one says that."

"I just did," she said with a head roll and tossed a long wave of brown hair back over her shoulder. "You need to calm down. Like, now. This isn't healthy and it definitely isn't going to impress the client. Did you get any sleep last night?"

"I got a little."

"Mr. Alexander?" The words rang out.

I groaned, knowing the owner long before I even looked up into those golden eyes. The sultry undertones of Eliza's voice had penetrated every sane thought last night, leaving me with nothing but the husky whispers of a woman restricted to pure fantasy I could never see through.

I shifted in my seat. Fuck. Even the sound of her voice was making me hard. How the hell was I supposed to work like this? She had to go. Right after this meeting, I would fire her.

God, that sounded harsh.

Who cares? You're used to making the tough calls. Work came first, didn't it? If I couldn't focus on my work, the only reasonable solution is to remove the source of the problem.

And what if *I* was the source of the problem?

"Here's the proposal form," Eliza said, leaning down to set the packet of papers on the desk in front of me. She turned to give Kinsley her copy and a part of her skirt brushed against my knuckles.

Immediately, my body responded. I was as hard as a rock and

ready to go into a meeting with a woman who held every last chance at redemption I needed in her capable hands. This deal meant much more to me than a business advantage. Hell, I wasn't making any money out of the deal at all. This was about repaying a debt too many years in the making to deny.

I needed her gone. Now.

"The pricing is listed on page twelve," Eliza explained. "And the bulleted point on page—"

I rolled my hand in an impatient gesture. "I got it. It's fine. Just ..."

Both women stared at me, mouths agape and eagerly awaiting the bullshit about to spill out of my mouth.

"Just?" Eliza cocked an irritated brow upward and crossed her arms across her waist.

"Take a break," I said. "Organize your desk. We'll be here for a while."

"I thought you wanted me to listen in and take notes."

"No. It's fine." I turned back toward the papers, pretending to sift through them. Anything to keep my attention away from Eliza and the way her skirt hugged each curve like a trial of temptation. "Kinsley is like a fucking recording device. We're good."

I kept my head buried in the paperwork, though I heard enough to know she'd left.

"Well, that went well," Kinsely said. "I can't imagine how you two don't make it through a day without killing each other."

"It's fine."

"You keep saying that."

"Can we just focus on the meeting?" I asked. "This is important, and I don't want to blow it."

This wasn't the first home I'd tried to buy like this in the past few months. It was merely the first I'd contacted about acquiring the property and the last one to respond. Not to mention, it was the most critical in making sure all the other gears set into motion functioned properly.

It would have been what Peter wanted, and I could, once again, sleep easy when it was mine.

"Everything will work out." Kinsley flipped through the papers in front of her. "It's a good deal with a good intention behind it. Though why you don't want to tell her what it's for outright is beyond me."

"People don't care about that stuff." That was all sentimental nonsense that had no place in a corporate setting. "They want numbers and data. Something that lets them know this is worth their time."

"I'm not so sure." Kinsley shook her head. "The fact that she's even meeting with you is a good sign on its own, but you just might have to adjust your usual approach. She isn't one of your regular clients, so you need to lay on a little more charm than normal."

"I don't know if I can do that." Charm? I had to be charming? I was used to hard negotiations, intimidation, and walking out whenever necessary to remind the client of the good deal they'd be losing by not signing.

But charming? I wasn't too skilled in that aspect, even when it came to women. That, too, was always something of a business transaction. She knew what she wanted and so did I. It was not about finesse or stupid notions like love. It was hot, primitive desires. Nothing more.

"There is a perfect gentleman in there, I'm sure," Kinsley said, standing as the door swung open.

I shrugged off the insecurities weighing me down, taking Kinsley's cue as Mrs. Montgomery entered. Now was not the time for uncertainty. I needed to focus, put on my most presentable personality, and plead my case for this property. "Maybe you're right."

～

She wasn't right.

The meeting was a complete disaster. All of the usual tactics failed to impress Mrs. Montgomery, and instead of folding, she put up a defensive front.

In fact, I was damn near sure she was only seconds away from telling me to go screw myself. Though as a seventy-year-old Southern woman, it was much more likely she'd say something like "bless his heart" rather than break decorum.

She hadn't done either. And in the end, she left without signing anything, completely convinced I meant to demolish two hundred years' worth of history and put up a concrete fortress.

"What the hell was that?" Kinsley asked, thumping me on the shoulder with a folder full of files.

"What was what?" Though I knew full-well what she meant.

"I told you to *adjust* your usual tactics. Be charming. Not go full speed ahead into your normal bullshit!"

"I tried," I said, even then I wasn't sure it was true. Had I really given it my all? Had I really done everything I could? Old habits died hard, and it was far too difficult to let my guard down about this.

"The hell you did," Kinsley said. "Why didn't you just tell her what you wanted the property for?"

"What good would that do?"

"I don't know." Her whole body shook, arms flailing wildly and eyes just as feral. "She might have actually considered you a human, rather than the snobbish asshole you were being."

I ran my palm over my face. This wasn't like me. If there was anything I knew, it was survival, adapting. These are all things I'd learned in the military and more. Yet, I'd embedded myself in this life for so long and treated everything like a cold, calculated purchase, I'd completely forgotten what it meant to interact with people on a personal level.

That opened up too many avenues for attack, exposing weaknesses I'd rather not make vulnerable. Kinsley handled all of the delicate matters. She was the charming one, while I was the enforcer.

Besides, telling Mrs. Montgomery why I wanted the property meant telling her about Peter. It meant opening old wounds and reviving ghosts better left dead. It meant admitting to deeds and mistakes that only made me seem less capable of running a business, less loyal ...

Less human.

"You need to fix it," Kinsley said, pushing me toward the door. "Like, now before she leaves. Tell her how important the property is and what it means to be there in that area. Just seal the deal."

It didn't take long to find Mrs. Montgomery, whose mad dash toward the door had landed her only a few feet outside my office. A twinge of panic seized my chest as I noted the object of her diversion. The woman was not only holding Mrs. Montgomery's attention, but my future in her hands as well.

Eliza.

Mrs. Montgomery released a hearty laugh and tossed her head back in amusement. Her sparkling eyes and broad smile illustrated the stark opposite features of the woman in the conference room. That woman looked at me with the same consideration someone gives to a flea. This woman, on the other hand, found nothing more delightful than Eliza Cortez.

The pleasant revelry faded as I approached, though the residue of smiles and laughter lingered. Eliza peered up at me with that same sweet smile she always wore, at least when we were around others.

"Mr. Alexander, what can I do for you?" Eliza asked.

"I was wondering if I might have a word with Mrs. Montgomery."

"I think I've heard all I need to, Mr. Alexander," Mrs. Montgomery said, still smiling and using a tone far sweeter than her words. "It's clear we are both after very different things, so I will stick with the current management of the plantation."

"You have a plantation?" Eliza asked, ripping the opportunity out of my mouth before I'd even formed the words.

Right on cue, Mrs. Montgomery turned toward her, eyes wide and bright once again. "I do. Been in the family for generations."

"I'd love to see it. I've always loved the architecture of Southern homes and the large sprawling grounds and the flowers." Eliza released a sound that was somewhere between a delighted sigh and a moan. Whatever it was, it shot straight to my cock, and I shifted anxiously in place. "It must be lovely."

Mrs. Montgomery tapped her hand against Eliza's desk. "Well, that settles it. You'll have to come visit."

Really? My fist clenched at my side. Not only was my presence being ignored, but my assistant was doing a better job at sealing the deal than I was.

"Was there something else, Mr. Alexander?" Mrs. Montgomery turned to look at me over her shoulder.

"I just feel like I didn't do our company justice in our intentions for this property," I said. "I'd really like another chance to prove this deal would benefit the both of us."

She passed a sideways glance to Eliza like she was actually fucking looking to my assistant for guidance. I was fucking done for; there was no way this was going to push through if she didn't say yes now.

"What do you think, dear?" Mrs. Montgomery said. "Tell me honestly. If he fires you, you can come work for me."

A smirk formed at the corner of Eliza's lip as she tilted her head to face me. Something twinkled in her eyes, fed either by pure amusement or the promise of revenge. "He has the right intentions for the property. His notes on the property suggest none of the physical structure will be altered in any way, with only moderate adjustments being made to the interior and landscape. I think you should hear him out on the issue."

"Is that true?" Mrs. Montgomery pivoted to see me, completely shocked and donning something close to admiration.

I nodded. "I have no intentions of tearing it down or damaging any part of the main structure."

"Then why didn't you say that in the meeting?"

"I ..." God, why hadn't I? It seemed like a pretty key selling point even before I'd started negotiating. "I guess, I was so focused on the data portion, it didn't cross my mind to discuss what I had in mind for the property. Usually, no one asks."

"Fine." Mrs. Montgomery moved toward me. "I'm not agreeing to anything yet, but I would like to invite you to the plantation for our annual Fall Masquerade next week."

"In Louisiana?" I sounded like an idiot.

"Well, that is where the property is located, Mr. Alexander," Mrs. Montgomery said, laying on the thick Southern accent with a mix of sarcasm and charm. "Is that a problem?"

"No. Not at all." *Yes, a huge fucking problem! How the hell are you going to go back to Louisiana without it being a problem?*

Had I actually thought I wouldn't ever have to go to the property? I mean, the whole point of buying this particular plantation was because of the ideal venue. But I hadn't thought about staying there for any length of time. A day trip out there and back would be plenty to sort things out once renovations began. No one would even notice my arrival.

Another ghost to add to their memories.

Maybe this gala would require only a day out of my time. It was just one evening after all.

"We can discuss the details when you arrive, Mr. Alexander. I'll set up a time for you to take a look at the property, and you can send over your ... notes, as well," she said. "Plan to stay a few days."

What the hell? The woman was like some voodoo mind reader. A few days in Louisiana. I was screwed. Things could not possibly get worse.

"Oh, and, Mr. Alexander." Mrs. Montgomery halted her exit to peer back at me. "Bring your assistant with you."

Chapter Seven
ELIZA

"What the hell did you say to her?"

Mr. Alexander asked, two seconds after closing the door to his office. Though I wasn't entirely sure why he was the one angry. If anyone should be angry, it was me. I was tossed out of the conference room like an unwanted puppy, a tragic and heartless act enacted by a man who was just as cruel. Not to mention, I'd practically saved his ass, and in return, he thought yelling and berating me should be my reward.

I hadn't even brought up the whole debacle from the night before, though I was fairly certain he hadn't forgotten about it either.

"What?" I asked. "I didn't say anything to her."

He planted both hands on his hips and leaned down toward me. "Apparently, you did because she's insisting I bring you with me."

"I talked about her shoes. I said they looked nice."

"You complimented her shoes?" he asked, unconvinced.

The man was so close to losing his life, and he didn't even realize it. "Yes. Surprisingly, people like it when you're nice to them."

"Don't test me."

"Or what? You'll leave me here?" *Don't test him! Don't test him?* The man had some nerve. All the while, I was slowly losing my patience.

"You had to have said something more than the shoes." He rolled his hand, as if expecting me to crank out more information on command. "Walk me through exactly what was said."

I shrugged and answered in my most sardonic tone possible. "'I love your shoes. Where did you get them?'"

"Very funny."

"That was it." I held out both hands before emphatically dropping them to my sides. "You know it isn't always about the deal, especially not in this case. People like Mrs. Montgomery care more about connections and legacies than they do about money."

"Everyone responds to money."

"She had plenty of it from what I could tell." The woman was wearing a pair of four-hundred-dollar shoes and toting a designer handbag worth even more. "It wasn't as important as having someone treat her like a regular person."

"Well, now thanks to your conversation, she expects you to join me on our trip to Louisiana."

I laughed. There was no way that was ever going to happen, for more than one reason. "I can't go with you."

"You have to come." His brow furrowed as he jerked his head from side to side as if he couldn't fathom the idea of anyone refusing him.

But I was refusing—hard. There was no way I could ever do something like this.

"I have my father to take care of. My family ... I just ..." There was no way. Who would take care of my father? How would my mom even be able to get to work? Even if it was possible for us to handle it financially, there was no guarantee Mama would be able to get the time off from work without jeopardizing what little of her job she had left.

Plus, there was the ever so slightest complication of my inexplicable fear of flying.

My stomach flipped. All the contents threatened to tumble forth at even the idea of climbing into one of those metal death traps. If I did go, we could take a car maybe? It wasn't such a horrible distance from San Francisco to Louisiana, was it?

"I can't do it," I said again, this time to myself.

"You have to. Eliza, this is your job," he said.

"I can't leave my father. My parents, they just wouldn't—"

"Is there no one else who can help you?"

"I mean ..." Maybe Gabi could come stay with them for the week. It wouldn't put her too far behind her studies, if at all.

No! This was what I had tried to avoid all this time. I had already sacrificed so much to allow my sister to do the same. I shook my head absently, letting my actions speak for me since the words lodged themselves in my throat.

"Eliza, I need you to do this." His hands wrapped around my forearms, reminding me of dangers I didn't want to explore. He shook me gently and tried to coax me from the pseudo-trance I'd found myself in.

I couldn't think clearly, not with his hands on me. Hell, I couldn't even think straight before he touched me. This could be an opportunity for me to advance my career, to make more money down the line. And yet, I felt frozen in place, unable to agree to anything and remaining silent.

"I need to get this property," Mr. Alexander said. "I'm willing to pay you extra for your time."

Extra? Did he realize how much extra that would entail? "You'd be paying me twenty-four hours for each day. With overtime over forty hours."

He didn't even flinch and only added, "I could pay you more."

"What?"

"Whatever you need," he said, completely sincere. "How is $10,000?"

My heart dropped. He couldn't be serious. How badly did he need this property? And for what reasons, if he was willing to overpay his assistant to get it?

"I need an answer, Eliza," he said. "I know you need the money. I'm willing to make it worth your while."

That kind of money would pay down the last of my father's medical bills. It would leave me with a buffer for a couple of months in case my mom lost her job. It was tempting, very tempting.

"How many days?" I asked.

"A week." He straightened, the smugness returning in full force. "We leave on Monday. So, you have the rest of this week to get what you need in order."

God, I was going to regret this. Nothing good ever came from making a deal with the devil. And I was signing away my soul to a man who'd wanted nothing more than to be rid of me only a week ago.

But I also couldn't ignore the benefits and all the good this trip would do in terms of finances and networking.

"Fine." I nodded and extended a hand toward him. "It's a deal."

~

I wasn't entirely sure what I was doing, only that I'd seemingly lost my mind.

Was this all really worth the $10,000 Mr. Alexander promised me? Was it worth my integrity or even my life?

Since saving time was crucial, driving to Louisiana was out of the question. He'd even laughed when I'd suggested it, as if it was completely unheard of for anyone to be afraid to fly nowadays.

So, there we stood, ten feet from the platform and only twenty minutes away from boarding. I was a nervous wreck to say the least. My body tensed every time the PA system sounded with innocuous information about a guest needing to head over to the gate or a final boarding call. To me, that sound heralded the announcement of something graver, like engine failure or a grounded plane.

Anything to remind me why getting onto that plane was the last thing on earth I wanted to do.

"Are you alright?" Mr. Alexander asked, his voice jolting me from my thoughts like a slap.

I shook my head, unable to fathom a reasonable excuse. "I can't do this."

"What? Go to Louisiana?"

"No." My fingers tightened around the handle on my

carryon. They trembled so furiously I feared I might lose my grip at any moment. "Get on that plane."

"I assure you, it's much safer than driving," he said.

"With a higher fatality ranking when a crash does happen."

He scoffed, taking a step closer. "Obviously. But much less fatalities overall."

"I have control over what happens to me when I'm driving."

"You have *more* control, not infinite control." He corrected me. "We never have total control over the stupid things people might do, even if we are careful."

Was that supposed to make me feel better? I pressed my hand against my face. I needed a drink or a valium. Anything to quell this feeling of anxiety clamping around my throat like a vice.

The first announcement for boarding came over the intercom permitting those requiring additional assistance to board the plane first. My teeth chattered. They actually shook up and down in my skull like some cartoon character in a freezer. I clamped down tightly to quell the ache, but it did little to stop it.

The lump in my throat swelled to the size of a golf ball. I could hardly breathe, let alone swallow. This was all happening too fast. Two weeks ago, I'd thought I was going to lose my job before I'd even been given a chance to prove myself. Now, I'd received an offer of a lifetime with the potential to grow in the field of my dreams. But only if I faced a fear that paralyzed me.

"Hey." Mr. Alexander reached for me. His hand stroked my arm tenderly and tugged me closer to him. "It'll be alright. I've flown hundreds of times. There's nothing to be worried about."

"You can't promise that this time won't be different," I said. "What if something happens?"

He shook his head absently, staring down at me with a knowing sense of pity. "Well, that's the question we all have to ask ourselves, isn't it?"

He stood so close, once again, despite all the times I'd pushed him away. If I wanted him to, he would kiss me. He would hold me, touch me, and make all of this go away. The subtle scent of his soap lingered in the air between us, warm and spiced with exotic ingredients only men of his caliber could afford. Every muscle in my body rallied against touching him, held me back from throwing myself into his embrace like a child seeking refuge from a storm.

He was still my boss. This would still be wildly inappropriate once we landed. And I would certainly hate myself for giving in to feelings I had no business entertaining.

"It's alright to be afraid," he said, "and to be unnerved by the feeling that nothing is in your control. But how we respond to those emotions is what matters most."

"And how am I supposed to do that?" I asked, the words barely a whisper.

His cool gray eyes assessed me with a compassion that did not register. This was not the man I was used to, the man who yelled and swore and threatened my very livelihood with every breath he took. This was an entirely different person. Someone I could almost convince myself cared about me and my feelings.

But then, that was absurd. Wasn't it?

"Take a deep breath," he said.

I stared blankly, still frozen. Not only did the dizzying grip of fear immobilize me, but emotions of confusion and desire slowly took hold.

When I made no move toward his command and remained silent instead, he did what I'd tried so hard not to. His arms came around me, slowly, hesitating, as if he anticipated my refusal at first. As soon as they encircled me, I realized how foolish I'd been to deny myself this feeling for as long as I had.

He felt wonderful, strong, and powerful in a way that made me feel safe. I breathed in his aroma and listened to the hypnotic pace of his heartbeat against my ear. All of it settled into me like rays of sunlight on a wintry day.

"Go ahead." His words brushed the top of my head. "Take a breath and count back from ten."

I inhaled slowly. My pulse fluttered uncontrollably, no longer led by fear but something else entirely. He was right. All of this took my mind off the flight, though not for the reasons he might have thought. Still, no matter what effect being so close to him had on the rest of my body, I sank deeper and deeper into the comfort his own offered. I didn't want to let him go. I didn't want to be cured of one affliction only to mourn the loss of his touch.

What was happening to me? I'd never needed a man quite like him. And it made the least amount of sense possible. He was off-limits in every sense of the word, but he was also a horrible human being. We couldn't have been more different, and yet ...

"Feeling better?" he asked.

I pulled back enough to peer up at him. All the pressure in my throat from before fled, replaced now by the drumming of my racing heart. The nausea induced by thoughts of boarding the plane shifted into twisting, churning waves. I didn't feel sick anymore; that much was clear. Though what I was feeling still proved completely foreign to me.

"I feel ... different," I said softly.

His hand rose to my forehead, brushing back a stray strand from my face. He watched me, regarding me like a phenomenon he couldn't make out. I wondered what it was that made him stare. What about me even fascinated him at all?

"Different how?" A dry overtone clouded his voice, as if he struggled with the words almost as terribly as I did. The twisting in my stomach bloomed into aching. One that demanded satisfaction rather than a cure.

God, I wanted this man. I'd spent years guarding my virginity like some treasure in a quest only one man deserved. I'd told myself only love would ever be enough to tempt me, then spent the greater part of my adult life pretending to be too busy to pursue it.

I still wanted love. I still wanted a grand romance foretold in fairy tales and novels. But I never wanted to give in to temptation quite as much as I did with this man. What would one night hurt? He could show me what sex was like. He certainly looked like a man who knew what he was doing. And I wouldn't feel so foolish when I came across a man I really liked.

I would actually know what I was doing.

No. This was stupid. The man would likely hold anything that happened between us like ammunition against me. Every time I told him no in the future, he would remind me of that one time I'd said yes. It wouldn't matter if the squabble was over something as simple as a coffee mixup or a repeat of our tryst. I could never go back from any of it. I would forever be his.

"I'm better. That's all," I said, removing myself from his

arms. I lifted my bag up over my shoulders and flipped the last few hairs out of my face. "We should get ready to board."

He nodded, a soft smile playing at his lips. Perhaps he knew as well as I did that it was only a matter of time before all my newest fears were confirmed.

I would give in to this man eventually.

And there would never be any going back.

Chapter Eight

JUSTIN

There were about twenty different things that could go wrong, though my concern centered nowhere on the state of the plane. If we went down, it would still be a preferable fate to the possibility of running into my parents.

How long had it been? Five years? Ten? I couldn't even remember anymore. All the years blurred after basic training. I'd simply put my head down, done my duty, and then moved on to the next project.

I'd made it home only twice the entire time I'd been stationed overseas. After Peter's death two years into our assignment, I never could make the journey back.

Too many places reminded me of him. Too many memories lingered in his absence, far more terrifying than any ghost. I could see it in the faces of those who knew him, how they blamed me for his death as if I had been the one to set off the detonator.

They had every reason to hate me.

All their glares and sneers, I deserved every one of them. The cold shoulders that said they thought I could have done more, I *should* have done more, I deserved that, too. Ten years, and I hadn't even heard so much as a word from the small group of friends I used to call my extended family. And the only time I'd ever heard from my family was on birthdays and Christmas. I never went back home and never made an attempt to reconnect.

Peter would have known all the right things to say. He would have told a grand, heroic story about how he'd carried me to safety on his back with a blur of chaos falling apart around him. Peter was charming in all the ways I never could be.

It should have been me.

"I can't do this." Eliza squirmed beside me. The shock on her face when I turned toward her revealed she hadn't meant to speak out loud. "Sorry."

"It's fine." Anything to take my mind off its current train of thoughts. I reached down and took her hand between my fingers. "Remember to count."

"I'm ..." A tremor pulsed through her. I noted the shaking in her jaw, and her inability to make out even the simplest of sentences. This was no basic fear. She was absolutely terrified.

I raised her hand to my lips, pressing a soft kiss there that stole her breath. She stared back at me with the same sense of wonderment and confusion she often did, as if she didn't believe the sincerity behind my advances or didn't trust her own desires. Hell, I didn't blame her. I wasn't even sure what I wanted from her. I wanted her. That was it. For how long, or to what degree beyond the sex, I wasn't sure.

Pursuing a relationship with my assistant was out of the question. Especially someone who spent so much time arguing and chastising me every chance she saw fit. But I could convince myself a good fuck was all we needed to get this tension out of our systems. Maybe, she wouldn't be wound so tightly afterward.

The only thing I knew for sure at the moment was that touching her was the best way to get both of our minds off of our concerns.

"It'll be ok," I said, holding her stare with mine. The warm glitter in her bewitching gaze appealed to me with something shy of childlike innocence. She was still afraid, but somehow sought comfort in me. A sense of pride welled within me. I liked that she found my touch as soothing and distracting as I found hers. Even after she'd pulled away, I couldn't chalk everything between us having been up to my imagination. I knew she felt something; I knew she wanted me. She just didn't want to admit it.

I reached forward and brushed back the chocolate strands encircling her face. She was beautiful and unlike any other woman I'd ever met. Everything about her set my body on fire. It had me tense and needing immediate reprieve. Even something as simple as holding her hand or holding her gaze made me as hard as fucking rock.

This was bad, very bad. Not to mention inconvenient. I couldn't afford a new assistant. With Kinsley constantly reminding me how difficult it was to find one who tolerated my many disparaging qualities, I knew how difficult it would be to locate another one in an expedient amount of time. And I was finally getting used to the way Eliza did things.

No, I did not particularly take to being given orders by my subordinate or having her give me any sort of critique at all. But it was preferable to having no help at all, and her demands were not all that unrealistic. In fact, things had become somewhat more efficient since she'd forced changes in our routine.

The plane pitched midair. She'd managed to make it through liftoff by watching me and employing a few long breaths. Only now, she jolted and threw her hands against the window at her side.

"*Madre de Dios,*" she said, though not so loud as to be heard by the remaining members in the first class cabin.

I laughed softly. "Do you speak Spanish fluently?"

Her eyes shifted to the side to see me, this time keeping her focus straight ahead. "Not as well as my father would like, but I do know all the necessary phrases and curses."

"That's helpful," I said, with a chuckle. "Where is he from?"

"Peru."

"His family..."

"Is still down there," she said, a note of regret in her voice. At least now, she wasn't trembling as much. Instead, she looked almost subdued.

"They haven't come to see him?"

She shook her head. "It's complicated. My father is too sick to travel, and my aunt is in her late seventies. She can't really make the trip."

"Have you ever been?"

Her eyes scanned the floor for answers, as if the truth lay there instead of the recesses of her mind. "No. All the extra money I've had either went to school, to help my parents, or pay past due medical bills."

I nodded, mulling over the information I already knew in an attempt to understand the woman beside me a little more. I knew she hadn't finished school from her file, likely as a result of her father's illness. Surely, the $10,000 would at least help with some of the bills and alleviate some of the pressure. Though knowing Eliza and her need to control every little aspect of her life, she would likely save as much of it as possible in the event of a crisis later on.

I watched her. What was it about her that fascinated me? She made me want to remember every unimportant detail about her life. Why? Because that's what she would do? It was all a tactic, I told myself. I was a ruthless negotiator, a businessman, and a soldier through and through. It was in my nature to collect as much intel about a person as possible to learn the most effective plan of attack.

So, did that make us enemies? Maybe I was simply asking all these questions about her to understand her more. Anything to get a leg up in our relationship. Because as of now, she was the one holding the reigns, even if I was the one signing the paycheck.

A sound chimed overhead, and we both looked up at the now unilluminated fasten seatbelt sign. Eliza removed her hand from mine and unhooked her belt. "Excuse me. I'm just going to freshen up or ... something."

I stood as she moved past me into the aisle. I tried to ignore the feel of her body as she pressed against me. Her hip brushed against my leg, and what little restraint I had left ground down to one fine, frayed tether. A throbbing ache pulsed through my cock, tempting me with visions of Eliza lying naked beneath me.

What must her body feel like? How did her lips taste?

I was growing too attached.

It was a dangerous transaction we'd already embarked on. Being this close to one another for so long, knowing how I felt about her, and knowing there was even less time and space between us than usual was like setting a wolf before a lamb. Even with all my years of training and discipline, I couldn't withstand the torture for much longer.

After five minutes of waiting, I began to wonder what had happened to her. We were virtually alone in the first class cabin, with only a few scatterings of single riders and couples here and there. She wouldn't have had to wait in a long line.

Another ten minutes went by and worry took hold. What if she'd gotten sick? What if she was in there hyperventilating and unable to move?

I unbuckled my seatbelt and headed toward the back of the plane. There was no line outside, there was hardly anybody in the area. The flight attendants distributed drinks to the other passengers, and a small curtain separated the restrooms from the rest of the cabin.

I knocked gently on the door.

No answer. My heart rate quickened. If I had to kick down this door ...

I knocked again and added softly, "Eliza, it's me. I just want to make sure you're okay."

A small pause followed, though eventually the door cracked open. She peered out at me, joining me on the other side of the door with a hint of trepidation.

"Everything's fine," she said. "I just wasn't feeling well."

My hand flew to her shoulder, protective. "Do you feel dizzy? Nauseous?"

"No." Her fingertips grazed her forehead, almost as if she might faint despite her claims. "It's just all very overwhelming."

"You'll have the rest of the day to relax when we land," I explained. "Then we can—"

The plane rocked, slamming her back against the door. I lurched forward, bracing myself against the wall beside her head and trying not to crush her. My head snapped down to see her, worried the turbulence might set her into some sort of panic attack. Her delicate fingers gripped the center of my shirt, and her eyes darted in every which way around the cabin.

When they landed on me, however, all uneasiness stopped. Intensity clouded the softness in her golden eyes, darkening like pools of honey or amber stones. A straight, soft black strand of hair fell across her face. Instinctively, I brushed it out of the way, leaving my hand to rest at her throat. Her lips parted on a sigh. That day in my office, I'd been so ready to kiss her. She'd even looked at me with that same hungered gaze, like she'd wanted me just as badly as I needed her.

But without any reason, she had turned away. Probably because she was infinitely smarter than me when it came to understanding the boundaries of a business setting. Only now, she wasn't pulling away, and I was slowly losing the battle to keep my hands to myself.

"Are you alright?" I asked.

She nodded and tilted her chin up to me. "Yes. Just a little shaken."

My thumb trailed along her jawline. It would be so easy to end this. So easy to answer all the lingering questions between us with one kiss.

"Fuck it," I grumbled beneath my breath and brought her mouth to mine.

To my surprise, she did not hesitate. Her lips met my kiss

with as much tension and need as my own harbored. Within seconds, I was lost. Lost to all reason, all sense. Lost to anything that reminded me this relationship could not be more wrong.

She tasted of spice and sunshine, like a strong swig of amaretto. Every movement left me even more intoxicated than the last. I needed more. As much of her as she was willing to give. I just knew, without a doubt, one kiss was not going to be enough.

My hand moved to her waist, holding her tighter against me. I wanted to feel all of her, the swell of her breasts beneath her blouse and the full curves of her hips stretching the fabric of her skirt. I wanted to be between her thighs, to know how wet her pussy was already, and give her pleasure she'd never be able to forget.

My thumb flicked upward, teasing the underside of her breast. She shivered and emitted a soft sigh in response. I was already hard, my cock ready to bury itself deep within her feminine folds until she begged for release. But I still had no idea what she wanted. Most of the women I bedded made their intentions known right from the start. They didn't scold me and argue with me on a regular basis. They either told me what they expected from our relationship or made no attempts to hide it.

I pressed a kiss against her throat, dragging my lip along the soft curve beneath her jaw. She even smelled like sunshine, like a soft green meadow of flowers. She was much too pure for me and much too feisty compared to my typical tastes. And yet, I needed every last part of her.

"I want to kiss you, Eliza," I said.

"You already have," she whispered, her words a mangled clutter of gasps and longing.

My hand rose to cover her breast, delighting in the subtle squeal she made as I gently squeezed. "I want to kiss you here."

The throbbing in my cock intensified. God! I had been hard since we'd boarded the plane. I wouldn't last much longer if I didn't take her now. My body rocked forward, pressing against her hot pussy beneath her skirt. A whimper escaped her throat, one of restrained desires just waiting to surrender.

"I want to touch you there," I said. "I want to make you cum, Eliza. Will you let me?"

She peered up at me, half stunned and half consumed with the haze of yearning. Her breasts rose upward on shallow breaths, and her hands clenched around the clump of my shirt still wedged between her fingertips. "I'm not sure."

I bent down and laid a kiss at the corner of her lips. "What aren't you sure about?"

"How far you plan to go."

"As far as you want me to. I'm not forcing you. I'm asking what you want." That couldn't be more clear. I wanted Eliza Cortez with every breath within me. But I was not about to take a woman who had no interest in me. My lips hovered above hers. Her breath dusted across my lips as she contemplated my request. "Do you want this? Do you want *me?*"

My mouth covered hers once again. Every flick of my tongue whispered of pleasures yet to come. Every move she met with equal passion. I ground my erection against the sensitive place between her thighs. This time, a moan emerged, muted by my kiss but vibrating all the way down to my core.

"Yes, dammit," she said, breaking free from my lips. "I want you."

I hauled her body up against mine and kissed her. A squeal of shock leapt past her lips. She quickly softened and looped her arms around my neck. She felt perfect against me, every bit as wonderful as I'd imagined and more.

I opened the door to the restroom behind her and helped her back inside the small room. My hands quickly set to work undoing her blouse, drawing the edges from the top of her skirt and tugging the two halves apart. She wore a lacy white camisole underneath, one that clung to her curves and exposed the tops of her breasts with an erotic allure.

Damn, she was beautiful. Everything about her captivated me.

My mouth trailed down her shoulder blade, feathering kisses along her skin until stopping at the lacy barricade. I glided the strap of her camisole down her shoulder. Within seconds, her round breast peeked out from the clothing, and I enjoyed every inch of the view.

I rolled my thumb over her tight, dusky nipple. She shivered beneath me, releasing a sigh like music from the heavens. It took every last shred of decency within me not to hike up her skirt and fuck her senseless. Two weeks was a long time to want someone without being able to have them, at least for me. I'd never had to wait longer than a day or two. Now, I wondered if all the waiting is what made this moment with Eliza so special, or if she just made me feel this way all on her own.

My mouth closed over her nipple, just as sweet as her kiss if not more so. I took the tight little bud between my teeth, laving and sucking until she writhed beneath me. Her hips bucked against my cock, and I almost lost myself completely. My hands clenched around her hips and pressed her back against the door.

"You've got to be more careful, Eliza," I whispered against

her nipple. She shivered from the mix of heat and moisture, and my own body responded with an inexplicable heat. I was damn near ready to give in, and I'd barely even touched her. "Another move like that, and I might not be able to take this slow."

"I don't care. I feel like I'm going to explode." She shook her head, panting. Her fingers laced through my hair, drawing hypnotic circles along my scalp. "I need you now. Please, I can't wait any longer."

I smiled despite the subtle warnings going off in my head. The ones that promised problems in the near future, those that had less to do with bedding my assistant and more to do with becoming too attached. Eliza was special. There was no denying that. But I wasn't falling for her. I barely knew her.

So, there was absolutely no reason to worry.

Was there?

Chapter Nine

ELIZA

This was bad, very bad, and yet I couldn't convince myself I'd done anything wrong.

I'd wanted this man. God, I'd wanted him forever it felt like, no matter how hard I'd tried to deny it.

And now, here he was, worshiping my body like the temple of a fertility goddess.

The thrumming between my thighs persisted. A mix of firm pressure and light pleasure, I needed it satisfied—now. I whimpered in impatience, knowing how hard he already was. I knew he wanted to get this over with as badly as I did, to finally pacify the aching we'd felt since the day we'd first met.

At least, that's how it felt for me. Ever since he'd touched me, I'd known I wanted him. I'd warned myself this was a mistake, tried to stay away. But it was all nonsense. There was no trouble in wanting him, in engaging in some meaningless flirtations and a little bit of sex as long as I didn't actually follow through with the entire act.

Right? At least, not right now.

I had held onto my virginity all these years, for what? Waiting for love to come swoop me up and carry me off to some magical feelings place. That wasn't going to happen. Not anytime soon. Maybe never. There certainly wasn't any time for a man in my life at the moment. I didn't want to be that person who saved her maidenhead like a precious gem, only to never use it at all.

But at the same time, this man was the last person on earth who deserved it. Justin Alexander was rude and arrogant. He made me angry and frustrated with so much as one look.

He was also devastatingly handsome and possessed a body forged by the gods. Not to mention his kiss inspired wicked thoughts, like jumping my boss in an airplane bathroom.

His hand cupped the back of my knee, gliding upward to the edge of my skirt. I trembled with anticipation. God, I needed him more than air at this moment and not just because of the confined space.

His other hand encircled my waist, holding me in place against him. I twitched as his hand grazed my inner thigh. His knuckles stroked along my womanhood, right where my lace underwear acted as the last remaining barrier between us. I had never hated an item of clothing more than that moment.

He stroked a fingertip along the curve of my underwear. He followed along the edge before stopping at my hip and tugging them down over my legs. The sensation sent ripples of bliss through my body, wrapping me in a soft blanket of longing I could not fight anymore.

Within seconds, he coaxed them over my heels and tucked them into an interior pocket of his blazer. The moment he touched me, all the pressure building within me shattered like glass. Ecstasy wove through me like a thousand tiny currents of light, warm and invigorating. He slid one finger inside me, and I nearly collapsed in his arms.

I reached out for him, steadying myself against his embrace. The hand around my waist moved to my back, looping around me to hold me steady. My knees weakened beneath each stroke, forcing the pressure to build within me all over again. Only this time, it felt warmer, heavier. It felt like a thousand pounds more weight constricted against my core, ready to explode in a fissure of rapture.

A web of heat scaled up my cheeks. All I could hear anymore was the thrumming of blood in my ears, our strangled breaths, and the faint words of Mr. Alexander coaching me to my climax.

Mr. Alexander. Is that what I even called him anymore? Had I somehow upgraded to calling him Justin? Nothing had really changed between us in terms of our position. He would still be my boss, and I would still be his subordinate. Only now, I had given up the one bargaining chip I'd still held between us. How would he take me seriously knowing I'd given in to his touch, knowing I still would again?

He slid another finger inside me and I cried out. *My God!* Had I known lovemaking would feel this wonderful, I would have pursued it more fervently a long time ago.

His lips closed over mine, swallowing another cry of pleasure as his pace intensified. I felt myself slowly unraveling. Searing waves of delight consumed me, spreading throughout my body until every limp went numb.

"Say it," he whispered against my brow.

"Say what?" I asked.

"My name."

Had he somehow read my thoughts? Were my feelings so obvious across my face, even to him? Maybe all this time he'd felt the same way about our relationship.

"Justin." His name crossed my lips like a prayer. Saying his name felt so intimate, so forbidden. It was as if I was glimpsing at a side of him, I would not otherwise be allowed.

Another thrust and all the ties holding me in place snapped. It was unlike anything I'd ever felt. It was warm and weakening, all in one.

He withdrew his touch and leaned against me. "I've wanted to do that for a while."

I laughed lightly, still breathless and unable to form any coherent thoughts. His eyes met mine with a mischievous twinkle, and a curve formed at the corner of one of his lips. "What?"

"We have a lot to discuss when we reach the hotel."

Something fell from my throat down to the pit of my stomach. What such a thing could be was completely beyond me, though the sensation was as unmistakable as the wrenching in my gut. He wanted to discuss things? What did that even mean? I was fired, quite possibly. Now that he had gotten what he'd wanted, there was no reason to deal with my stubbornness and perfectly rational requests, which he deemed outlandish.

Maybe he wanted to take things further. Did I even want to take things further? I didn't not want to, I guess. I just always expected more for my first time. I'd expected more commitment, more love, more of an attachment than pure unadulterated lust.

"I thought I was going to be able to relax," I said.

"Do you not feel relaxed now?" he asked, with a wicked grin.

He wasn't wrong. I felt almost dazed, tired. I felt like I could finally take a nap on this metal death trap until we landed.

"I would feel better if I had my underwear back," I said and reached for his blazer to retrieve the item in question.

He pulled back and held his hand over the pocket. "No. That's not going to be possible."

Horror gripped me. "What?"

"I'm keeping them for now," he said. "You can have them when we get back to the hotel."

"You can't be serious." I was supposed to sit there without any underwear for the remainder of the trip. The very idea elicited a gentle throbbing between my thighs yet again. My God, was this actually turning me on? Did he have plans for me going commando the rest of the trip, or was this just some sort of ploy to humiliate me?

"Very serious," he said, pressing a kiss to my lips before pushing me toward the door. He opened it and shoved me outside into the aisle. "Now, out. I have some things to take care of."

Then he slammed the door closed and left me alone to find my seat.

The remainder of the flight carried on without as much enter-tainment as the first half of the trip.

I'd fallen asleep against the window almost instantly after returning to my seat. I had floated in and out of consciousness on waves of dreamlike slumber until we'd landed. I was only vaguely aware of Justin sitting beside me at times, calmly pouring over forms and folders filled with information I'd plied him with regarding the Montgomery Estate.

It was actually quite a big ordeal. The masquerade ball Rosalie Montgomery had invited us to was a long standing tradition that dated back to the late 1870's. Every year, the wealthiest and most powerful people in the South attended, with the occasional guest or two from the outliers of Southern society to join in the festivities. And every year, the costumes and decorations became more outlandish than the last.

I'd never been to an event that dictated a formal dress code like this. Beyond graduations and prom, I'd never needed to wear a fancy ball gown, nor had the dresses for those occasions been anything notable. I hadn't even had a quinceanera, and I was now expected to pretend I was some highbrow lady in a society of fools.

Part of the extra time in Louisiana was to be spent getting ready for the ball. I was to meet Rosalie the next afternoon. She would approve of Justin's tux and take me to find a dress. That way, I'd have a few days for the alterations to be made before the party.

Me needing alterations like some bride preparing for her wedding. This was nonsense. How did I even get roped into all of this? I didn't even know where to start when it came to finding a dress, let alone how to act before a room filled with the country's elite.

"Are you alright?" Justin's hand closed over mine and I jumped.

We stood in front of the conveyor belt, watching it spit out unfamiliar luggage until it finally produced ours.

"Yes," I said. "Fine. Everything's fine."

"You're worried about the ball," he said, his hand still covering mine. "You don't have anything to worry about."

"That's easy for you to say. You grew up in this world of billionaires and hoity-toity nonsense."

He chuckled to himself. "You know it all, huh?"

"It's what's on your profile." I shrugged candidly. "Not hard to figure out."

"My company profile says I come from a family of billionaires?"

"Not in so many words."

He inclined toward me, his lips close to my ear. "And what if I told you, I don't?"

The heat of his words sent tiny shivers down my spine, recalling all the sinful things he'd done with that mouth and with his hands only a couple of hours before.

"What if I told you my parents are humble people who didn't want any money, even after I'd made it?" he asked.

My eyes narrowed. What kind of people wouldn't appreciate financial help from their son? Especially one with so much disposable income as Justin Alexander, real estate mogul and hotel tycoon? True, not everyone needed millions of dollars to be happy. They may even see it as a burden. Yet, something in his tone intimated a much darker secret. Like those only a man who'd had to make hard decisions harbored. No one could doubt Justin was a tough negotiator, but nothing in his success screamed of ill-gotten gains.

"I would have to wonder why," I said finally, suspiciously.

The laugh that followed sounded more like a scoff than a form of amusement. He was hiding something he clearly wanted to share but had no idea where to start.

Now was not the time for such intimate conversations. We could finish this once we reached the hotel when we weren't surrounded by any number of prying eyes and ears.

"What else did my profile say?" he asked after what felt like an eternity of silence as he collected our luggage from the carousel.

I shrugged one shoulder upward, unsure how much to infer about his character. If you'd have asked me two weeks ago what I thought of the man, it would be a very different portrait from the one I now held. He was constantly changing, constantly surprising me. I liked things to stay as they were, to have one sound judgment about a person to rely on. But Justin Alexander was an enigma I couldn't quite unravel. As soon as I made one assessment of his character, he would strive to prove me wrong.

"It was just information about the company," I explained, gliding my suitcase along behind me as we searched for the exit. "You acquired your first hotel at the age of twenty-two, a bed and breakfast actually, which you later converted into a small series of chains. You spent four years in the marines, stationed overseas mostly and grew up in a small town in the South but don't have much of an accent."

"The military tends to beat it out of you," he said flatly, a soft smile already forming. "And it was eight years in the marines. Four years active duty, four years in the reserves. I was actually deployed once during that time. Kinsley had to take over for me."

He stared straight ahead, a stern unyielding in his gaze that was as cold and pensive as always. Only this time, I noted the uneasiness in his body. The tense shoulders, the way his hands flexed around his luggage handle. Did he want to share more? Did he want to share his secrets ... with me?

"You always do your research before taking a job?" he asked suddenly, passing a sideways glance in my direction.

"When it's something this important, yes."

"You always wanted to be an assistant?"

"No," I said. "I want to work in the hotel industry."

"Why haven't you?"

"Too many things going wrong at the same time, I suppose." That was the simplest way of putting it.

"Your dad?"

I nodded, touched he even remembered. It wasn't important for him to remember things like that, things that fell outside of his duties as my boss. Even our brief interlude didn't guarantee he cared about anything more than himself. Though it certainly hadn't felt that way.

"Once he's feeling better and I can save up more for school, I'll go back," I said. "And after this week, at least, I'll be another step closer to saving up for that."

He smiled and emitted something along the lines of a laugh. The good humor in his features quickly faded as we exited the loading area into the outside world. His stare landed on an older couple, possibly in their late fifties, early sixties. Each one held a side of a large poster board that had "Welcome Home" on the top and "Congratulations" on the bottom.

"What is it?" I asked, unable to read the meaning behind his quizzical brow.

"It's my parents." His hand pressed against my back, guiding me toward the adorable couple with the sign.

"Your parents live here?" It all made sense. Why he so

desperately needed to seal this deal, why he loathed the idea of coming here in the first place. What didn't make sense, however, is if he hated his hometown so much, why even bother building a hotel here in the first place?

"Yep. And it looks like we've been ambushed." His smile broadened as he approached his family, almost cartoonish and too insincere to be taken at its face value.

It didn't matter to the couple holding the sign. His mother practically jumped up and down in place in anticipation of throwing her arms around her son. She was not the type I would have imagined for his mother. Though there was nothing lacking in her polished and refined features, a warmness exuded from every inch of her like an embrace. She probably smelled like apple pie and owned a home with rocking chairs on a veranda overlooking a bayou or stately sequoias. Everything about her felt like home.

"Welcome home," the older gentleman beside her said, extending his hand out to Justin. A burst of pride welled up within him. He was tall and trim with only the slight paunch of a belly from what looked like years of enjoying beer. Nothing about either of them screamed shame.

So, why had he always treated the idea of family as a pestilence to be eradicated?

"What are you guys doing here?" Justin asked.

"We heard you were coming, and we wanted to surprise you," his mother said, then leaned over to give me a hug. "Welcome, sweetheart. I'm Debbie and this is Bob. We're so excited to have you here."

"Thank you." I forced a smile. What the hell else was I

supposed to do? This all was so surreal, I couldn't even make sense of it.

"What's the 'Congratulations' for?" Justin asked, motioning toward the sign.

His mother flashed a charming smile and knowing stare, before chucking him gently on the cheek. "As if you didn't know. Come on. Everyone will be waiting for you at the house."

"Everyone?" Justin stopped her. "Waiting for what?"

"Your engagement party," she said, completely serious.

My first thought had been, he's engaged? My second lingered somewhere along the lines of how I'd committed pseudo-adultery with a man ready to walk down the aisle with another woman. But the reality was far worse than I could have ever imagined.

His mother turned to me and gently squeezed my arm in affection. "Welcome to the family, sweetheart."

Chapter Ten

JUSTIN

"*H*ow the hell did this happen?" I shouted into the phone.

It had been thirty awkward minutes stuck in a car with Eliza glaring daggers at me the entire way.

I hadn't corrected my parents. How the fuck was I even supposed to clear up something like this? I show up unannounced for the first time in ten years, and they think it's to surprise them with the love of my life. They even hatched some brilliant plan to throw an engagement party for the two of us to show there's no hard feelings or bad blood left in the wake of my thoughtlessness.

I wanted to make amends. I was seeking the whole community's forgiveness after what had happened to Peter. If I told them this was all some misunderstanding, it would only rub more salt in the wounds.

Once I took over the Montgomery Plantation, once I made my peace with all of this, they would have something else to marvel over instead. I could say it didn't work out between Eliza and I. Engagements fell apart all the time. I just needed her to continue the charade for a little while longer, though I knew it would cost me dearly in the end.

To her credit, she'd played the part expertly, despite almost calling me "Mr. Alexander" twice and tensing anytime I put my arm around her. When she'd met my aunt and uncle, she'd recounted the details of the first day we'd met, noting how rude she'd thought I was but was slowly won over by my incessant attempts to win her back. And when she'd told my cousins about how she was initially put off by my affinity for porcelain dolls and the collection I'd amassed in my converted garage over the years but grew to love me anyway, I knew I was as good as murdered the first moment we were alone.

"I'm just as shocked as you are," Kinsley's voice came in through the receiver. "To think, all this time, you were sitting on such a juicy secret. I'm appalled. Especially since you seemed to be against her so much in the beginning."

I grit my teeth. Were all the women in my life completely insane? "It's not true, Kinsley. I swear ..."

"Oh, please." She scoffed. "I saw the photos. You two were practically making out. I almost had to break out a cigarette after seeing it. What did you think people were going to imagine?"

"Very funny," I said, and scrolled through the article on the computer screen in front of me. A photo of my arms around Eliza in the airport consoling her filled the screen. By all accounts, it did look a lot steamier than it actually was. Though even I had to admit, it meant more to me than I realized.

It didn't mean we were engaged!

The fucking media. Anything to sell more papers. I'd kept myself out of the tabloids for years, only allowing carefully crafted stories and features to leak out into print. It was only natural the one time I slipped, the press was all too eager to report on what billionaire Justin Alexander was really hiding.

"I just need it fixed," I said and closed out the window on the computer.

"What's there to fix? You two make a lovely couple."

"Kinsley, don't test me. I need you to find out who the photographer was, who reported on it, and have them both killed." At least they had kept Eliza's name out of all of it. There wasn't a clear view of her from the photo, and she wasn't someone the press would immediately recognize anyway. Though it was only a matter of time.

"You're probably closer to them than I am," Kinsley said. "Why don't you take care of it?"

"Cause I am currently attending my engagement party." Or at least I was in the same house as the engagement party. Currently, I was hiding out in one of the empty guest bedrooms of my parents's historical bed and breakfast, which housed upwards of twenty different rooms for rent. Not the Ritz, mind you, but a nice respite for anyone wanting to enjoy the old world charm of the South.

Kinsley laughed so hard I think I even heard a snort escape through the other end of the phone. "So much for keeping your return home low-key."

"Yeah, thanks for the reminder." I cracked open the door and peered out at the guests in the common area. Still no sign of Eliza. They'd been like wolves surrounding us, tearing at us from every direction until I'd finally lost track of her in the swarm of people. "It's not like I'm not trying to navigate a crowded bed and breakfast that is clearly over capacity while worrying about my reputation as a professional."

"Well, it should make you feel a little bit more at ease to see so many people turn out for your homecoming," Kinsley said. "What did Eliza say about all this?"

"She hasn't said much to my face. Though I'm sure I won't make it past tonight if we don't find a way to fix this."

"What do you expect me to do?"

"We need to take control of the narrative." The last thing I wanted was the corporate world thinking I was fucking my assistant. I'd look like some reckless idiot who couldn't keep it in his pants long enough to make rational decisions.

Not to mention the backlash Eliza would get. They'd call her a gold-digger and a social climber. All her aspirations about rising to the top would be ruined before she even started. No one would take her seriously with a history like that—even if it wasn't true.

"What do you want me to do?" Kinsley asked.

"I don't know. We need some sort of cover story," I said. "One that sounds better than 'Billionaire Fucks His Secretary.'"

"She's not your secretary."

"They won't see it that way. Anyone in my employ they'll make out to be the equivalent of a whore." I shut the door, satisfied no one had yet seen me and unable to locate my supposed fiancée. "Eliza doesn't deserve that."

"Aww." The saccharinely sweet tune of Kinsley's voice wove through my ears like a melody. "You like her."

"Don't be stupid. I just don't think she should be subjected to the same scrutiny as we are." Kinsley had been the victim of bad press once or twice in her lifetime. The media was far crueler to women than it was to men. She had to know what something like this would do to someone so inexperienced with the process like Eliza. "You know what they'll do to her when they find out who she is."

"What do you suggest?"

"Get someone from public relations on it. I want them to publish a counter story. Something that paints the two of us in a better light than this."

"Do you still want to be engaged?" Kinsley asked.

Now that was the million dollar question. For now, the engagement detracted from all the painful feelings and all the ill-will my family and friends felt toward me in my years away. A few more months and the foundation would be up and running, or at least well underway. I'd have something else for them to remember me by, something else that would make up for all the wrong I did in the past decade.

If Eliza and I parted ways amicably by then, who could really fault me?

But I hadn't even discussed the matter with her yet. Who knew how long she was willing to keep up this ruse?

"Have them come up with a few ideas for me, and I'll run them by her," I said.

"Run them by who?" The door shut behind me. "*Dearest.*"

I turned toward the entrance of the room just in time to see Eliza lock the door. She was pissed.

"Kinsley," I said into the phone. "If I'm found dead tomorrow, tell them my wife killed me."

Eliza ripped the phone from my hand and put the speaker to her lips. "Don't bother. They'll never find the body."

Without hesitation, she hung up the phone and tossed it down onto the bed.

"What the hell were you thinking?" she asked. "You ambush me with something like this and just expect me to jump through hoops for you. Why on earth would you tell them we were engaged?"

"I didn't. Someone took a photo of us at the airport and made assumptions."

"It was a six hour flight," she said, "including the layover. How the hell could news spread so quickly?"

"I am always in the spotlight, Eliza. It isn't unheard of for people to try to dig up dirt on me and spread ridiculous rumors without checking the facts. My mom, apparently, gets notifications anytime someone writes something with my name in it, and lo and behold, this came up."

She glared back at me, arms crossed over her chest and completely unconvinced. "And I'm supposed to just believe your mother put together this whole celebration in less than a couple of hours."

"The woman has run a thriving bed and breakfast for the past thirty years with only my father's help," I explained. "I've learned not to put anything past her at this point."

"And every one of your family and friends just happened to be available?" she asked.

"It's a small town." And not everyone had made it. Peter's parents weren't there. Peter's sister was supposedly on her way, along with Sawyer and Harrison. All of which I could endure another lifetime without seeing again.

"That doesn't change the fact that you need to fix this."

"Don't think I'm getting any enjoyment out of this," I said. "You told my cousins that I select a different doll from my collection each night so I can wash her with baby oil and brush her hair for twenty minutes. Even *I* needed therapy after hearing that story, and that's not even counting the shit I'm going to get from them about it."

She jammed a finger in my chest and uttered something in Spanish that sounded more like a curse than a compliment. "You told them I was your fiancée! Clearly, you can see how wrong that is to force on someone. Especially someone who works for you."

"I didn't realize this was going to happen."

"You didn't do anything to tell them otherwise. Maybe I should do it for you. I can go out there right now and say 'Haha. This was all a big joke. I can't even stand the sight of him, let alone accept a proposal of marriage from him.' Would that work better for you?"

"It's complicated."

"More complicated than pretending you're married to your assistant?" she asked. "What happens when they find out the truth?"

She was making all valid claims. But even the thought of disappointing these people yet again was enough to make my stomach turn. I'd withstood two tours in Afghanistan and negotiated deals with some of the toughest clients in the corporate world. But this was something I couldn't do?

What is wrong with me?

"We just need to pretend we're together for as long as necessary and then, part ways once the housing project goes through," I explained.

Her eyes narrowed. The ridge in her brow formed a tight *V* in the middle of her forehead. "What housing project?"

"The one I'm here for."

"The Montgomery Plantation?" She scoffed. "That's what this is all about?"

"More or less. Look, we don't have much time to discuss all of this before they realize we're both missing. Just ... if you do this, I'll make it worth your while."

She looked offended at first, but then, money had prompted her to come on this trip with me in the first place. Everyone had their price. And Eliza needed the money just as badly as anyone.

"And I suppose you'll want all the extracurriculars that go with being a fiancée, too," she said, her voice noticeably shaken.

Fuck. I'm an asshole. I hadn't realized she'd be worried about something like that. Where did we draw the line? We'd already come close to fucking earlier on in the day. Given just a little more time together, we'd eventually forget ourselves and dive headfirst into passion. But now, it would feel too much like I was paying her.

I didn't want her to feel obligated to sleep with me or to feel like she owed me anything other than the requests I made now. I wanted her to want me because she couldn't imagine being with any other man. I needed her to feel the same agony it was standing so close to one another without touching.

Only now, all of those lines blurred.

"I'm paying you for the appearance of a fiancée, not paying you to *be* my fiancée," I said, slowly closing the distance between us. "So, unless you plan on having sex with me in front of the entire family, I don't think that'll be necessary."

She blushed and turned her head to the side to deflect the

effect of my words. I tipped my finger beneath her chin and brought her attention back to me. Her eyes declared a silent war, faltering only once when they landed on my mouth. Every breath crossed her lips like a sigh. A dreamy haze overtook her, though she quickly stamped it down.

"But I can't have you blushing every time someone brings up the idea of us being together, either." Absently, my thumb traced her bottom lip. Despite all her anger, the lingering remnants of desire remained in her gaze. Sleeping with her might be out of the question, but I couldn't have her tensing up everytime I held her hand or brought her against me.

I leaned into her, dusting my lips along her temple. My hands claimed her waist, exploring her curves like uncharted territory that belonged only to me.

"I will have to touch you," I whispered against her brow, "and kiss you. All the normal things a couple does when they're in love enough to get married. And you sure as hell can't keep calling me 'Mr. Alexander'."

She didn't move. The only change in her entire body was the rapid incline of her breaths. "How long?"

"For as long as we're here," I said. "Things can go back to normal when we get back home, then, I'll wait a few months to tell them it's over."

She nodded weakly. "Fine. It's a deal."

Chapter Eleven

ELIZA

$\mathcal{W}$e suffered through the remainder of the introductions for another two hours after our conversation. Needless to say, I was too exhausted to care that we'd traded in our two separate rooms at the local hotel for one shared bed in his parents' bed and breakfast.

I fell asleep within minutes. I didn't even change clothes or put on a fresh pair of underwear to replace the ones still in Justin's coat pocket. It still felt weird calling him by his first name instead of Mr. Alexander. It felt strange sleeping in the same bed as him and pretending all of this was a completely normal thing that people did when they'd only been employed for two weeks.

We'd settled on two hundred grand. He was to keep his distance, except for the usual kiss or touch in public to sell the romance. But other than that, whatever weakness occurred between us the morning before was to be a thing of the past, something forgotten and never repeated.

It was better this way.

We were playing a dangerous game as it was. We didn't need any other complications insisting their way into our lives, blurring the lines between fantasy and reality.

We reached the boutique where Rosalie told us to meet her, a small shop with diamond-encrusted dresses displayed in the window. It was the best place in town to get the most magical gowns suited for a fairytale ball. But even with a two hundred thousand dollar boost to my salary, I was a little leary to purchase something so extravagant for one night.

"Eliza, you look lovely, dear," Rosalie said, greeting us almost instantly as we crossed the threshold. She took my hands in hers and gently kissed my cheek. When she pulled back, there was a knowing sense of mischief in her gaze. "I hear congratulations are in order."

"You heard about the engagement?" I asked. Though I wasn't entirely sure why I was surprised. Anyone keeping tabs on Justin would know of the engagement. Hell, anyone in this small Southern town had likely heard about it already, considering we'd met half of them last night anyway.

"Yes, well you know the rumor mill is quite strong down here, darling," she explained. "But I didn't pay it any mind until I read the announcement in the paper this morning."

"The announcement?" I turned to look up at Justin, who kept his gaze straight ahead.

He shifted on his feet, then pressed his hand into my back. "Yes, pumpkin. We talked about this last night."

"Of course, *payaso*," I said sweetly, reaching up to tenderly touch his cheek. His eyes narrowed, possibly gathering by the tone in my voice that *payaso* was not a real term of endearment. "But I didn't know we were going to announce it so soon."

He inclined forward, wrapping his arm around my waist. The physical contact completely threw me off guard, and I faltered in maintaining our already waning veneer as a couple. He tapped one finger against my nose, and I resisted the urge to smack him. Rosalie was watching, and per our new agreement, I had to pretend to be in love with him.

The devilish smirk on his lips revealed he knew exactly what he was doing and just how much pleasure it gave him. He leaned in further still, and added, "I didn't want to waste any time in letting the world know you're mine."

"You two are adorable," Rosalie said, sweeping her hands in a dramatic gesture of approval. "I'm going to go check with Bernice about our appointment today, but feel free to go ahead and start browsing through the dresses."

As soon as she moved out of earshot, I pushed Justin toward a row of dresses to finish our conversation. "You put an announcement in the paper?"

"I had to." He shrugged. "The press was going to turn this into some sort of sleazy affair. Now it sounds more rags to riches than anything."

"Rags to riches? So, now I'm the poor little charity case, and you're the prince?" Typical. I sounded like the pathetic damsel in distress, while the man came out as the hero.

"It's not like that, Eliza." He sighed, rubbing a hand along the back of his neck. "Both of our reputations were at risk. I didn't want anyone thinking I was screwing my staff, and you sure as hell don't want anyone to think you are making your way up the ladder the hard way."

"So, what *is* the story?"

"We've been dating for a while, and when I had trouble finding a new assistant, you stepped in to take over temporarily," he explained. "Working together made it difficult for us to hide our relationship any longer, so we made the announcement formally."

"Oh. That does sound good." It definitely made the most sense. I sounded more caring than conniving in this version at least. The fact that he'd even taken my reputation into consideration at all was surprising. Almost touching. "Thank you."

"No problem, pumpkin."

I groaned. Of all the names. "Don't call me that."

"Not a fan?"

"No."

He chuckled, toying with a piece of material on one of the dresses. "I thought as much. Probably the same way I feel about being called a clown."

Whoops. So, he did know what *payaso* meant. Not surprising. With his track record in business, he likely found himself called much worse in half a dozen different languages. I pivoted away from him, busying myself with the row of dresses and pretending to be as interested in looking through them as a blushing bride. "Technically, it's more like a buffoon."

"A buffoon?" He laughed again. "Who even uses words like that anymore? You and Kinsley should form a club. Fine. What terms of endearment am I allowed then?"

I shook my head. Did I want him to call me anything sweet? Diving down too deeply into this narrative put much more than our reputations at risk. There were plenty of couples who didn't use pet names. It didn't make it essential to the charade. "I don't know. Just call me 'Eliza'."

"But that's your name."

"I'm very well aware it's my name, just—"

"Justin?" The voice emerged at the end of the row of dresses, along with two unfamiliar faces. The two men blocked the exit, the first much closer, while the other hung back. "Is that you?"

A flash of recognition spread across the first man's face, and he quickly extended his hand out to Justin. "It's nice to see you. Sorry, we didn't make it to the party yesterday. Pete's sister had a leak in her roof that needed my attention, and Sawyer ..."

"Didn't want to go," the man in the back said flatly. The muscles in his jaw twitched, and his eyes darted around the room for any source of distraction. When they fell on me, however, a softness replaced the cold irritation lurking beneath. He inclined his head in an act of reverence, and I felt the sense he was usually much more charming than he was at this moment. "Though if I'd have known your fiancée was so enchanting, I might have made the exception."

Justin cleared his throat. His hand lightly pressed against my back as he gestured toward the two men. "Eliza, this is Harrison and Sawyer. I went to school with them."

"Pleased to meet you," Harrison said, with a smile that exuded comfort rather than charm.

The two men could not have been more opposite, both in dress and appearance. Harrison, undoubtedly the sweeter of the two men, wore a simple pair of jeans and a button-down shirt with rolled sleeves. His reddish-blonde hair and ice-blue eyes matched his angelic, down-home Southern appearance. Whereas Sawyer looked more like the Devil himself. Dark, brooding, and sporting a jaw peppered with day-old stubble, his expensive suit stood as the final fixture in his role as the infamous deal maker.

"What are you doing here?" Justin asked.

Harrison shrugged. "Charlotte asked me to pick up her dress for some event this weekend."

"The Montgomery Masquerade?" Justin asked, a little more suspicious than before.

"You're going?"

"Of course, he is," Sawyer said. A wicked grin curved his lips at one end, and he released a not-so-subtle scoff. "Word is he's been after the plantation for a few months now, but Mrs. Montgomery wasn't too impressed with his negotiation style."

The hand at my back flexed. I peered up at Justin, though he kept his glare firmly settled over Sawyer. "Why are you going?"

"Sawyer buys and sells real estate," Harrison explained. "I restore the properties, especially the older ones. We even have a few bed and breakfasts outside of town that we've built up over the years."

"I had no idea you were in real estate," Justin said. What he really meant was, this had now turned into a competition.

"Yeah, well, you miss a lot of things when you drop all contact with everyone for over a decade," Sawyer added, delivering a blow that even I felt. "You're not the only one who's made a name for himself in the hotel industry."

"No. I'm just the best."

"And on that note, gentlemen," I said, pushing past them, "I'm going to see if Bernice is ready for me."

They were children! Absolutely immature and only one misplaced word away from brawling right there in the shop.

Though the conversation did raise one of two questions I bookmarked in my mind for later.

Like, why had Justin stayed away from home for so long?

And why return now?

~

It took all of five seconds for Bernice to tell me my proportions were not that of a normal woman.

My waist was a size two, while the rest of me was somewhere between a size six and eight. Genetically equipped with hips made to bear children, I already knew a dainty dress was far beyond the realm of possibilities. Yet another reason I hated shopping for fancy dresses. They either made me look pudgy or way too sexy for a formal setting.

Even when it came to events like prom, I never saw the appeal. All the other girls would have a major glow up, with hair and makeup accenting their features perfectly. Not me. Instead, I looked and felt completely out of place.

I was on dress number seven when I decided this was the last thing on earth I wanted to be doing. I liked the color at least, a deep, sapphire blue with glittering rhinestone embellishments. It tumbled down my hips in smooth, satiny splendor, reaching the floor in a soft pool of material.

It would be difficult to dance in, but at least it wasn't a very long train.

You need to choose something!

I fumbled with the zipper on the back. Dresses always looked different once they were zipped. And this one was already a little snug as it was.

I peeked my head out the door to flag down someone for assistance. Instead of Bernice, Justin stood outside the door, his head buried in his phone and scrolling through what looked like puzzling information.

He looked up at me as I pushed open the door. His eyes scanned what little of me extended past the door, questioning the look of concern and confusion on my face. "What's up?"

"Where's Bernice?" I asked.

"She's helping another client. What's wrong?"

I looked past him, searching for anyone other than this man to help me. "I need someone to zip up the back."

"Here." He coaxed me back into the dressing room. "Let me."

"Wait ..." Any protest was short-lived. The door swung back into place behind us, bouncing softly against the latch before closing completely. I peered into the mirror, watching his large form behind me.

It was a simple enough task with very little in terms of intimacy to recommend it. But any contact from him set my skin alight in ways I still wasn't prepared to handle. One hand slid around my hip, holding me in place as the other brushed my hair over my shoulders. Shivers wove through me where his touch met bare skin.

I was near trembling by the time I heard him say, "There. Already done."

The woman in the mirror no longer looked so sure of herself. Not that I was the pinnacle of confidence and grace to begin with. I had resigned myself to getting the dress, purely out of the need to be done with trying them on in the first place. Only now, I wasn't so sure.

The dress clung to my figure like a second skin. Maybe if I wore pantyhose beneath it or Spanx, it wouldn't look so unappealing. Anything to smooth out the lines and make me feel a little more comfortable.

Then again, maybe it was best to wear something loose and darker. Something that attracted far less attention than this.

"You look incredible," Justin whispered against my ear.

I met his gaze in the mirror. "It's not too tight for a formal setting?"

"No. I like the way it fits." His hands closed around my waist, smoothing along the silken fabric with a touch as placating as it was possessive.

I watched him touch me, let him explore every dip and curve, absolutely mesmerized. My body tensed beneath him, led by feral instincts that told me both to run and to stay. His lips embarked on their own journey, across my cheek, my neck, and down my shoulders.

This was wrong. All of it. We had a deal to keep things simple. No touching outside of the necessary requirements. And yet, here we were, awakening feelings better kept below the surface. He knew every trick to draw me back in, every tantalizing temptation designed to lure me into his arms.

"Are you going to get the dress?" His breath feathered across my cheek.

I slid my eyes closed, trying to focus on anything other than how wonderful he felt. "I might."

"You need me to help you take it off?"

I tensed. Good God, the man knew exactly what to say to throw me off. "I need you to *unzip* me."

"Same thing." He brushed my hair to the side, placing a kiss where the exposed skin met the hemline. The zipper gave way easily, and with it, I felt a small part of me unraveling as well. Why did I subject myself to the torture? Why did I deny something I so clearly wanted?

Because you promised to keep him at arm's length. Men like Justin Alexander were dangerous. They thought nothing of romancing a woman, winning her heart, and leaving her to pick up the pieces later.

His fingertips slipped under the sleeve of my dress, gliding it down my arm in a tantalizing path.

"Justin ..." I whispered, turning over my shoulder to see him. My words lost all protest when his lips touched mine, enticing me back into his embrace like a woman who relished the threat of heartache.

I didn't. But good Lord, he drove me wild.

My hand struggled free of the dress sleeve, and I reached behind me to drag him closer. He tasted of sweet, forbidden desire, like an apple from the Garden of Eden. With just a word, I might give him everything. I certainly wanted to. But the two-hundred-thousand-dollar payout made me question the integrity of a billionaire who'd rarely been denied anything he wanted.

We'd agreed our arrangement did not include sex. But that didn't mean he wouldn't still expect it. In the end, I stood to lose far more than he did: my pride, my virginity, and my heart.

His palms closed over my bare breasts. I hadn't even realized I stood halfway undressed before him. "God, Eliza I need you. Right now."

I struggled for breath in between every kiss. I needed to take control, remind both of us how nothing could ever really happen between us. "We had a deal."

"Fuck the deal," he said and pressed his forehead to mine. "This has nothing to do with it. I know you want this."

His hand slid down my stomach, coercing the knot already forming there to tighten. When his roving touch finally found the sensitive space between my legs, it took all restraint not to cry out in surrender.

"God, Eliza. You're so ready for it," he whispered against my temple.

The world around me faded to stars and blinding pleasure. I was damn near close to letting this man sex me up right here, in a public place. Again.

It would be different if I were an experienced woman, driven by sex, and absolutely content with nothing but the physical pleasure I'd derive from a brief moment with this man.

But I wasn't. I never had been. I wanted love, connection.

All things Justin never could give me.

I shoved his arms away from me, breaking his hold over me in more ways than one. "That doesn't mean it's going to happen in a dressing room stall."

I moved to the opposite side of the tiny room and collected my clothing. Any amount of distance between us proved pointless to us thinking straight. Within seconds, his large form was behind me, the heat radiating off of him like a bonfire.

"But it *will* happen." His words rumbled against my ear.

A tremor wove its way down my spine, driven as much by desire as it was anticipation. "We're getting the dress."

Chapter Twelve

JUSTIN

othing was going to plan.

Within 48 hours of stepping foot in my hometown, I'd acquired a fiancée, a rival to Montgomery Plantation, and the makings of a serious headache. Not to mention, I was in no way closer to purchasing the property than I was six months ago.

Being here brought back too many memories and too many painful ghosts better left undisturbed. Some of the waking nightmares that kept me awake weren't even from here. They belonged to a time I'd struggled hard to forget, to move away from. But being here triggered them all the same.

The only thing that kept the phantoms at bay and the only person who seemed to bring reason to all of this madness was Eliza.

But even she had kept her distance from me for the past two days. Every time I had asked her for her help in settling business affairs, she'd always provided some excuse about plans with my mother or Rosalie. Yet somehow, whatever I'd asked her for would still magically appear on the antique desk in our bedroom later that evening.

She was avoiding me. Not that I blamed her. We'd both been emphatic about the terms of the agreement. She didn't want me overstepping any boundaries, and I certainly didn't want her to feel like she owed me anything.

But I could not get the woman out of my mind. I needed her with every last breath within me. A concept I found more and more disturbing as the days passed.

What happened when all of this was over? Would she move on to something else? Someone else?

Would I never see her again?

The door opened and Eliza walked inside. She froze the moment her eyes landed on me sitting across from her on the bed.

"You're here," she said flatly and closed the door behind her.

"This is our room."

She shrugged uneasily and moved toward the small dresser near the bathroom. "Well, you are always out so late."

A pair of high heels dangled between her fingers. She cast them to the side and set to work unlatching every piece of jewelry on her body, placing them in a dish on the dresser.

"Where were you?" I asked, noting the tight fit of her clothes as opposed to her usual business attire and the remnants of makeup. She looked fucking amazing. But I was not the one she'd dressed up for this time.

I grit my teeth. Why the hell did that bother me?

"Out with a client," she explained.

"What client?" Clearly, she was lying. Though why she felt

the need to hide anything from me was yet another irritation I couldn't handle. "The only client you know here is Rosalie, and she and I were out discussing the new proposal."

"He's a new client."

"He?" A niggling ache wrenched its way into my gut. I was by no means a jealous person. I'd never needed to be when all previous arrangements had founded themselves on sex alone. Eliza was different and always had been. It was pointless pretending I hadn't secretly claimed her as mine weeks ago.

"Sawyer." The name crossed Eliza's lips like sandpaper grating along a chalkboard.

If I hadn't already been convinced of my inclination toward jealousy when it came to her, this definitely solidified it.

"Sawyer is not a client." I all but spat the words. "He's competition."

She tugged her blouse out from the top of her skirt and lifted it up over her head. Only a thin camisole remained in its place, tucked into a black skirt that clung to her waist and hips. A hundred images of past, present, and fantasy blurred into one, and I nearly forgot our conversation completely.

"He asked me to meet with him," she continued, unaware of the current course of my thoughts. "He wanted to discuss potentially withdrawing his bid, provided he saw evidence that the plantation was going to good use and not being dismantled."

Now it made sense. Sawyer was a businessman. He wouldn't shirk from a deal on merit alone. He wanted something in return. Though in this case, his terms were not negotiable. "He wanted evidence. Right. And what evidence did he request? You lying naked beneath him?"

Eliza's glare bore into me from across the room. In all my

years of screwing people over, I'd never once encountered a look so murderous. Nor had I ever troubled over it until now.

"You, of all people, have no right to say that to me," she said.

Perhaps, I didn't. But it didn't change the reality of the situation. "I'm not blind, Eliza. I saw the way he looked at you. You don't know Sawyer like I do. You wouldn't be the first married woman he's enjoyed chasing."

"*We* are not married," she said, gesturing emphatically between us as if to prove her point. "Nor will we ever be."

"Yes, but Sawyer doesn't know that. Instead, he'd think nothing of screwing you to get to me."

She closed the space between us. "Because that's what this is all really about, right? You and your little revenge plots."

I stood, meeting her power stance with one of my own. "Stay away from him, Eliza."

She inched her chin higher, defiant. "Or?"

Fuck. Or what? Was I going to threaten her? Fire her? I wasn't that deluded to think I could control anything Eliza did. No matter how badly I wanted to, I had no say in who or what Eliza wanted.

"There is no 'or', just ..." I sighed, defeated, and reached for her. She let me. Her body pressed against mine, every line falling into place perfectly. "Please, I don't want to see you get hurt."

"He's not the one I'm worried about."

A dull ache pulsed in the center of my chest. It pressed against my lungs, suppressing all breath and rational thought. "You think I'm going to hurt you?"

She set her jaw and shifted her head to the side. "You already do."

Bullshit. She was imagining the pain long before it even

began. I hadn't hurt her. I hadn't even so much as looked at another woman since I'd met her or given her any indication of running. She was simply scared by her own feelings and what a legitimate relationship like ours might really be like.

Hell, even I was scared. But Eliza was worth it.

"I want you, Eliza. There is no hiding that," I said. "Though I can't promise you a life with a white picket fence right off the bat."

She pushed me away, placing a few feet of distance between us. "I'm not asking for an eternity. I just want something real."

"You won't know if it's real because you refuse to let me in."

"Letting you screw me in a public place is not the same as shutting you out," she snapped. "It's being practical."

I reached for her, drawing her up against me and forcing her gaze to hold mine. "Then now."

"What?" Her eyes widened, half in fear and half hampered curiosity.

"One kiss, right now." The edge of my thumb grazed her lower lip. She shivered, her eyes turning that bewitching shade of caramel honey. "You tell me when to stop."

My lips brushed hers, not waiting for an answer. I let the gentle movements entice her. Each caress reminded her this was not uncharted territory but a rhythm she knew as well as her heartbeat. Slowly, her lips parted beneath mine. They offered more, demanded more. Without even knowing it, she was lost.

And so was I.

My hands closed about her waist. Every inch of space between us ate away at me in acute torture. Her breasts pushed against my chest, thinly protected by her almost sheer camisole.

Instinctively, I touched her, testing the boundaries of how far she'd let me take one kiss.

I could wait an eternity for Eliza, though I was certain it was the furthest thing from her mind. She'd already given in, and that's what scared her most. That despite all the warnings in her mind, this was a battle already lost from the beginning.

It was a feeling I knew all too well. Though it was safe to say I didn't know what I even expected from our relationship anymore. I just wanted her. Was that so wrong? I wanted to feel her beneath me, enveloping me. I wanted to hear her cry out from pleasure only I could give her.

The dull thrum of my cock signaled the collapse of my slowly waning restraints. Fuck! I was already rock fucking solid, and I had barely even touched her.

My hand dove into the silken strands of her hair, cradling her delicate skull in my palm as I slanted my lips over hers. A sudden release of need overpowered us both. She twisted her hips, sending her sweet pussy against my cock, and I went damn near numb trying not to toss her onto the bed in response.

My fingers crept along the hem of her skirt until I found the zipper in the back. It gave way easily, parting and sliding down her hips until it fell to a pool of cloth around her feet.

"You said one kiss," she whispered against my mouth.

I froze, my hands still on her hips and awaiting her response. "Do you want me to stop?"

"No," she said. "I just think you knew we could never stop at one kiss."

With a gentle tug, she dragged her lips hard over mine, completely unaware how badly her words affected me. One kiss would never be enough. One *night* would never be enough.

Though I was still far from legitimizing this arrangement with any declarations of love, I couldn't help but wonder if this was what falling felt like.

The remainder of our clothes joined the slowly growing pile at our feet. I guided her back toward the bed and laid her down against the soft collection of blankets and decorative pillows. My hands continued their exploration of her body, unsatisfied by chaste kisses and tender caresses. I needed her now; I needed to be inside her.

My mouth closed over her stiff, dark nipple. Her body arched in response, and she released a moan of pleasure so sweet that I nearly lost all control. The last thing I wanted to do was rush this, but I could feel every last tether snapping. Two weeks of foreplay had to be some sort of a record. No man could withstand torture like not. Not a man who'd grown accustomed to getting everything he wanted in an instant.

I moved down her stomach. Her muscles clenched beneath my lips, flexing and flinching as I brushed against her. When I kissed the inside of her thigh, every inch of her tensed.

"Justin." Her voice was a plea. "I feel like I'm going to burst."

"Shh." I blew against the sensitive crux of her thighs, reveling in the gentle twitch of her body as her pussy begged for the attention it deserved.

My arms hooked beneath her legs and drew her to the edge of the bed. I knelt before her and slid a finger between the silken folds. She reacted immediately, writhing beneath my touch from sheer pressure alone.

Good God! She was so tight. My cock throbbed in impatience, wanting to be where my hand was, to fill her completely until I had ruined her for every other man.

Because she had ruined me.

It took only a few quick strokes, and Eliza was already on the precipice of breaking. My tongue joined in the intoxicating dance, swirling about her tiny nub, sucking and flicking until she could scarcely hold still.

"Oh, God, Justin." Eliza's hands gripped my shoulder. The pinch of her nails digging into my skin brought with it a whole new sense of eroticism. Not only did a little pain add to the pleasure, but she was damn near begging me to take her. I needed to hear it. Needed to know she wasn't going to take it back the second I was inside her.

Or regret it later.

I wanted all of her, but only if she wanted me in return.

She let out a curse as she crested her orgasm. Her grip weakened as she relaxed against the mattress. I slowed, letting her coast down off of the high rather than pulling away. She was panting, one hand pressed over her chest as if to quell her racing pulse.

I leaned over her, brushing a strand of hair from her face and pressing a kiss to her lips. "Eliza, tell me what you want."

She nodded, still shaking. A resolute determination swelled in her gaze, fueled by desire and feelings long suppressed by our pride.

"Yes," she said. "I want you. All of you."

Our mouths found each other, falling back into the soft rhythm of comfort meeting yearning. She was not a one night stand, not someone who knew our relationship was built on sex alone. She felt like home, love, and everything I'd denied myself for too long.

I guided the tip of my cock to her entrance, easing in to let her get used to me before all primal urges took hold. She bucked her hips upward, and I sank deeper inside her. A rush of heat surged through me.

Fuck. So much for taking things slow.

I pressed forward, sinking further until finding that magic spot of ecstasy. Her lips tore from mine, and she bit her lip to stifle the cry forming. Every sound she made drove me crazy and encouraged me further until we fully lost ourselves in pursuit of ultimate bliss. With each thrust, her body contracted around me, leading us both closer to pleasure even I'd ever thought imaginable.

It had never been this good. And Lord help me, I had no idea why.

I sure as hell wasn't going to last much longer. My pace quickened, watching the feelings of rapture heighten within her features. She tumbled over the edge, gripping my shoulder and releasing another moan of surrender. I followed shortly after, unable to hold on any longer.

"Fuck," I cried out, practically collapsing over top of her.

Next time, I'd last longer. Next time, I'd give her every ounce of pleasure she deserved.

Would there even be a next time?

I had just slept with my assistant. No, my fake fiancée.

The woman I had happily paid two hundred thousand dollars to walk away from me without qualms after all this was done. There was no guarantee of a next time, no matter how badly I wanted it. We had only two days left in Louisiana, and things would return to normal, whether I liked it or not.

It turns out, I was the one who was screwed.

Chapter Thirteen

ELIZA

I woke up the next morning wondering what in the hell I must have been thinking.

I hadn't been drunk or drugged. No, this had been some other kind of intoxication. One driven purely by lust and curiosity that spoke to the virgin who wanted more.

I suppose this had always been what I wanted. Waiting seemed an eternity, a prison sentence I had placed on myself without knowing the end. Who knew if I was ever going to meet Mr. Right? What if I died an old maid without ever having sex?

Though to be fair, it had been much more than ordinary sex. Not that I had anything else to base it off of beyond crude explanations from friends. Still, the experience affected me deeper than the sheer mechanics of the act. Hell, after the second orgasm, I was positive I knew all the answers to the universe's questions.

It had to mean something, didn't it?

Maybe Justin didn't love me, but there was no denying the attraction I felt for him. Maybe ... even more than an attraction.

It was a thought I allowed begrudgingly to enter my mind. I wasn't in love with him. I wasn't even entirely sure I was falling for him yet. But if I had to make a mistake with anyone, give in to unrelenting desires with a man who didn't love me in return, it might as well be him.

All that was certain was two days from now, we'd be on a flight headed back home. We'd return to our separate lives, meeting only in a professional capacity, and I would have an extra two hundred thousand dollars to do with what I wished.

The only question was how long were we to keep up this charade? How long after we returned home did we have to wait before announcing our break up? And what would that mean for us in the workplace?

Good God. Everyone in the office would need to know. They likely knew already. So, what would they think when we returned to the office only to renounce the engagement?

Now, we were on our way to meet Rosalie. She was partly to blame for this whole mixup. If the deal did go through, it wasn't like we could just call off the engagement as soon as we returned home. She'd get suspicious. Hell, she already was suspicious of Justin and his hairbrained proposal for her property. No wonder he was having trouble competing with companies like Sawyer's.

"How long are we to be engaged?" I asked finally.

Justin turned to face me, nearly missing the color change of the red light to green as he stared awestruck. "What?"

"We never discussed how long this little charade is supposed to go on," I said, facing forward. I amused myself with the passing buildings, the incredible plant life, and small town,

Southern charm. These were all things you didn't get back in San Francisco and all things that distracted me from looking Justin in the eye.

"When we get back to work," I continued. "Are we supposed to announce it to everyone all over again? Or do we just pretend like nothing happened?"

Nothing. Absolutely no response followed from him for a full minute, which seems like a short amount of time, but it felt like an eternity.

His silence forced my attention back on him. He kept his eyes on the road. The only indication I knew he'd heard me was the slight twitch in his jaw.

"Well?" I asked.

He grumbled to himself. "Must we discuss this now?"

"Well, why not discuss it now? It should be a simple enough answer to come up with." I deserved to know what my life would look like. After last night, we'd crossed too many boundaries to leave it open without further discussion. I'd grown too attached, committed more than I ever expected to a man who might toss me to the curb the first chance he had.

I needed an answer. Even if it wasn't one I wanted to hear.

"Why don't you give me an answer," Justin said.

Oh God, no! That would be even worse. What if I said I wanted to take things slow, see where they led? What if I said I wanted more than a few days, and he simply laughed at the idea?

"I'm not the one who came up with the scheme in the first place," I said. "I thought you would have an idea of when it might end."

"First of all, it's not a scheme," he explained. "It was an accident that I hired a very expensive PR rep to handle for the sake of *both* our reputations."

I only vaguely knew about this PR rep. How else would he have been able to orchestrate such an elaborate story so quickly? "Still, you must have an end date in mind. We'll be going home in a couple of days, and—"

"Then we will discuss it on the plane," he said, the words practically a growl. "Right now, I just want to get through this meeting with Rosalie first."

"Fine." I threw myself back against the car seat in a huff. If he didn't want to discuss it, it was better I just assume everything would be over immediately after departing the airplane.

Neither one of us had even discussed the previous night. We woke as usual, got ourselves dressed and ready, then grabbed some coffee. It was almost as if we'd dreamt it.

But we hadn't.

No matter how completely fantastic it all sounded, no matter how wonderful he made me feel, I could never have imagined it.

He didn't want to discuss it now. Fine. I could appreciate the importance of keeping his head in the game for a meeting with Rosalie. He still hadn't been able to convince her why his need for the property mattered, and I was feeling less and less confident about my ability to dissuade Sawyer. But I sure as hell wasn't waiting for the plane ride home to discuss matters as important as how long he planned for us to be engaged.

We arrived at the plantation home shortly after, making the intense silence of the car ride somewhat less overwhelming. Large wrought-iron gates that seemed to stretch toward the sky opened onto a cobblestone pathway. A series of massive oak trees draped in moss and dangling tendrils of leaves lined the paved road, drawing the eye to one of the most beautiful homes I'd ever laid eyes on in my life.

It looked like something out of a fairytale or an old history textbook. One that elicited tales of ghosts and romance and danger. It must have had about fifty rooms, several acres of land, and a story worth telling. There was no surprise why Justin wanted it. Though what he intended to do with it was another story.

Even I had to admit, there were some things that didn't add up. He'd made his fortune acquiring properties, fixing them up or tearing them down to rebuild money-making locations. All of his other acquisitions consisted of hundreds of rooms and more commercial furnishings, like pools, gyms, and day spas.

There could still be room for a gym or a spa on a property like the Montgomery Plantation, I supposed. But it would never be anything like the elite level hotels of Alexander and Dawson Holdings.

Which only seemed to add to its allure. The only question was why Justin wanted it. Why this property above all others? There were other stately mansions in the South, some closer to more touristy destinations like New Orleans. For a man who hated his hometown so much and hated the idea of even seeing his family for longer than a week, he was bringing business far too close to home. He could have chosen any number of other locations, in several other states, with miles between him and his family.

But he chose this one. Why?

"Mr. and Mrs. Alexander." Rosalie descended the steps of a large veranda that seemed to have no end. She let out a soft chuckle as she said our name, clearly amused by some unknown joke.

"I suspected there was something going on between the two of you," she said, stopping to greet us on the drive. "A subtle, stolen glance or just an energy in the air. But now that I see the two of you together again, there's no denying it."

Unease wove through my stomach. Dear God. How many people were we going to deceive with this little ruse of ours? How many people were going to feel utterly disappointed and used if the truth ever came out?

Rosalie thought we looked in love. My eyes drifted to Justin, who remained focused on Rosalie and some over-the-top thank you for letting us see the grounds. He spared me no thought. He couldn't even discuss matters that concerned us both without getting irritated.

We looked in love. Hardly. If anything, we were two people who simply kept making one mistake right after the other.

"I would let y'all take a tour inside," Rosalie said. "But they are decorating it for the gala tomorrow, and it's just a lot of chaos right now. You'll get to see the interior tomorrow night. Still, I can show you around the grounds. Many of the oak trees here are older than the property, and there is a beautiful fountain constructed by my great-grandfather in honor of his marriage to his third wife."

Rosalie conveyed the last bit of information with a cheeky smile. She leaned in and added, "There's a bit of a scandal that went with all of it, you know? There's a lot of history and a lot of memories—all things I don't want to vanish with a massive overhaul."

"We don't plan on changing the structure of the home,"

Justin explained. "In fact, I'd like to preserve as much of the house as possible. There would only be some minor changes. But I chose the house for that fact that it seemed to encompass all the things needed for our project."

"Yes, your proposal discussed converting some of the rooms into multiple bathrooms," Rosalie said. "That seems like a lot of damage to rooms that have remained the same for years. Far too much change."

Justin nodded, staring up at the house as if imagining the changes he meant to put in place. "Well, it would only be one or two rooms, depending on the location. We could make it work, and you could have a say in which rooms are changed."

A wrinkle formed at the center of Rosalie's brow. She motioned toward a small footpath and guided us down what looked like the entrance to a fairytale garden. "I'm not a fan of change. I prefer things to stay as they are. I understand that is not entirely practical, but then, I have no real need to sell the property. Don't you agree, dear?"

Rosalie patted me on the arm. Dread squeezed the very breath out of me. What the hell was I supposed to say? This was not my place. Technically, I was still just the assistant. If I said one wrong thing, I'd be blacklisted from the industry by my very own fake fiancé.

I could do this. I simply had to remember what was in the proposal. What was the one redeemable quality about this whole endeavor?

"It's not just about selling the property," I said, thinking back to the clause about the plantation being kept as a non-profit rather than a commercial hotel. "It's about doing some good with it."

Rosalie perked up at that. She tilted her head to the side, and her stunning eyes bore a twinkle of delight. "How is that?"

I cast a sideways glance at Justin who did not look in anyway pleased by my assessment of the situation. *Crap!* I was screwed. But at least Rosalie looked happy.

"This property isn't meant to be held like any of the other resorts at Alexander and Dawson Holdings," I explained, treading lightly for fear of being murdered in my sleep. "We aren't converting it into one of the large conglomerate chains. We want it as is but to serve a more altruistic purpose."

"Which is?"

Damn. This was as far as I could go. Justin hadn't disclosed that much of his plan in the proposal or to anyone else it seemed. I looked to him, gesturing toward Rosalie to prompt his input. "Maybe you could explain it better than I can."

"Can I?" he asked. His eyes narrowed over me, though a sense of mischievous teasing flashed across his features. "We haven't narrowed down what the non-profit will be used for as of yet, but we do intend to use it for charitable purposes alone."

Rosalie stopped beside a large fountain, likely the very same one from the story she'd told. She looked out at the hordes of trees and pepperings of large hydrangea blossoms, still clinging to life in the last stages of bloom. "Why? What interest does a large company like yours have in charity work?"

"Plenty." He shrugged, as if the answer was clear. It wasn't. To anyone. "Not to mention it looks great come tax season."

"Cute," Rosalie said. "But how do you intend to fund all of this? I don't want this endeavor of yours to lead to the plantation falling into disrepair."

"We have more than enough funding to keep the property going."

"If this is purely altruistic, Mr. Alexander, why not choose something a little closer to home?" Rosalie asked, pinning him with a stare that stood somewhere between malicious and curious. "Something, in say, your own backyard?"

"This *is* close to home for me." Justin's words caught me off guard. I'd heard him pitch ridiculous deals before. I could tell when he was lying, when he was coloring truths for the sake of a negotiation.

This was not that time.

Not only did he sound absolutely sincere, something in the tone of his voice whispered of sorrow. Did he regret staying away for so long? Did he truly want to return to his family and want to try to make things work? Maybe he just didn't know how. He needed some sort of excuse to make the journey out here every so often. He needed something other than family, something even the workaholic in him could not ignore.

"Yes, I am familiar that you grew up here, Mr. Alexander," Rosalie said, still unconvinced by the emotions in his words. Whereas I was damn near ready to wrap my arms around him and tell him it was perfectly okay to cry. "But if the rumor mill in town is anything to go by, you've not been back in quite some time."

He tensed. That tiny muscle in his jaw twitched once again, and he shifted from one foot to the other. "Well, we can't always trust the rumor mill, can we?"

"So, you deny it?"

A pause. I could practically see the wheels turning in his head, trying to concoct some sort of excuse, some sort of reason for staying away for so long that made his answer more palatable to his audience. Instead, he simply shook his head, partly defeated and partly humbled. "No. I haven't been home in over ten years."

"Then, why here?" Rosalie asked. "Do you intend to reconnect with your family?"

This was opening up a whole new set of questions Justin was clearly not ready to answer. He was drowning, unable to commit to anything that involved his family—not that I blamed either party for their respective approach to the situation.

Rosalie had every right to ask about his intentions for the property. Family meant everything to her. Legacy meant everything. Preserving the integrity of the property was all that really mattered, not money and not progress.

Yet, somehow divulging any reason Justin wanted this property hit far closer to home than he let on.

So, this wasn't just some random acquisition. This wasn't something he hoped to use to revolutionize his company or to start something new. It may not have even been about family, since he couldn't seem to make up his mind about how often he would return. Either way, this was personal. And he was not yet ready to air that dirty laundry with the world.

"Justin has every intention of taking exquisite care of the property," I said, interjecting before the silence drove all three of us insane. "Right now, he's still nurturing his relationship with his parents and old friends, so it's hard to commit to an answer in that respect. He may wish to revisit the past, but there are others not so readily able to do the same."

Like Sawyer. I'd never seen a man hate Justin more than he did, which was truly saying something in the type of business

Justin did. You didn't get to be a multi-billionaire without stepping on a few toes. You didn't become head of a major hotel chain without squashing a few of the little guys and demolishing competition.

But with Sawyer, it wasn't business. It was personal. Whatever had happened between them hadn't been brought up at our meeting last night either. It was some grand secret everyone in town seemed to know about, but everyone refused to talk about.

"I see." Rosalie nodded, quietly musing to herself. "That makes sense. Though as you may have already guessed, family means everything to me."

She dusted a finger along the tiles of the fountain, as if drawing memories straight from the stones themselves. "A word of advice: Family is not always perfect. But knowing what's worth fighting for and knowing when to back down is the hallmark of a true gentleman. Only a fool or a coward backs down from something he can't live without."

Rosalie stood. She gripped my hand and squeezed it lovingly.

When she approached Justin, she pressed a frail hand against his cheek. "I wonder which one you will be."

Chapter Fourteen

JUSTIN

Fuck my life. If things got any worse, I'd be living on the fucking streets.

It didn't look good when the woman dragging her feet trying not to sell you a property all but called you a coward. And what was worse, she was right.

I was a coward.

All those years spent away from home. Did I really think they were doing any good? It wasn't everyone else I was worried about. If they saw me again, they wouldn't burst into flames. Harrison acted as though nothing had happened, even if he was avoiding me. Charlotte and her parents just avoided me altogether. In fact, they completely ignored my existence, so there was no real harm done on their part.

And if I was being honest, I'd have to say Sawyer enjoyed pissing me off. So, for him, my returning home was more a catharsis than anything.

It was me. I was the one not yet ready to face them. I had been the coward all these years, too afraid to face anyone. Not even my parents.

Every time I saw them, all I could imagine was the pain I'd caused and all the guilt I felt. It overwhelmed me in ways I didn't want to explore. It was much easier just to shut out the pain, to shut out everyone associated with it and forget all about how I'd let my best friend die.

"Are we going to talk about what just happened back there?" Eliza asked.

We hadn't even made it upstairs to our room, and I had no intention of carrying on a conversation like this out in the open. Hell, I had no intention of having it with Eliza ever.

She was the last person I wanted to know about all of this. It was enough that Kinsely knew my deepest darkest secrets. Kinsley didn't judge me. She had her own demons to fight.

Eliza was different. The woman probably never even stole a stick of gum from her mother's handbag, let alone did anything wrong of real significance. No. If I told her what had happened, she would never look at me the same again.

"We're not discussing it," I said and moved past her to the kitchen. I needed a fucking drink.

"And why not?" she asked. "You don't want me uncovering any dark, dirty secrets? Well here's a surprise for you. You may need to tell somebody what's going on from time to time. It isn't healthy to keep all of this bottled up."

"Kinsley knows," I said, flatly. "That's it. She's the only one who needs to know."

Eliza glared back at me. She only flinched once during my

admission that Kinsley knew more than she did, though she quickly recovered. I filed that information in the back of my mind, noting that perhaps Eliza could get jealous on occasion, too. Though now, was not the time to dwell on such observations.

"Then call her and talk to her about it." Eliza ground out her words through nearly clenched teeth. "Because all of this drama and ridiculousness is getting you absolutely nowhere with your property."

Fire swirled within my chest, collecting into a massive fireball of emotions. Was I angry, irritated, or just ashamed? I couldn't even tell anymore. All I knew was that Eliza was saying things that rang all too true. I was close to losing my property, the one that was supposed to fix all of this misery for me, as if this one act of veneration would atone for all my sins. It was more like slapping a Band-Aid over a gaping wound and hoping for the best.

But the last person I needed to hear it from was Eliza.

"Look, sweetheart," I said, leaning forward and closing the distance between us. "I appreciate you trying to take control of the situation. But this is not something you can handle."

She straightened, setting her jaw in the frustratingly determined way. "Only because you refuse to let anybody else help you. What is it? Why don't you want me to help?"

Good, Lord. The woman could never let anything go. Couldn't she see I was quickly losing my patience? It never seemed to stop her before. She was the only other person besides my feisty business partner who actually stood up to me. And that was when she was my subordinate.

Now ...

Well, now was she not? Despite everything that happened between us, had anything really changed? Maybe I was holding her up higher than I should. We'd slept together but that didn't mean she had any say in how my business was run or how my life was run. I'd never given any other women those liberties.

I had to make it clear. We'd gone on with this little ruse of ours for too long. We were both beginning to blur the lines of our relationship. "Despite what the title says, darling, you're not actually my fiancée."

"And thank God for that," she said, barely even moved by my words.

Fuck, did I really want to hurt her? It just didn't sit well in my chest that she was so unaffected by the lack of an attachment. Maybe she was doing a better job than I was at remembering where the lines were drawn.

"I would hope that the man I was about to marry would at least trust me with a little of his secrets," she added, "and with any part of his life. I just want to help you as your friend."

"Are we friends?" I laughed.

Silence followed. Glorious, maddening, deafening silence. I turned toward the cabinet and removed a glass bottle of whiskey. Hell, it wasn't even the good stuff, but who gave a fuck at this point? I downed a shot, took one look at Eliza, and determined I'd need the whole bottle just to survive the night.

Whether I'd be awake in the morning was another story.

I started down the hallway leading out to the backyard. Thank God my parents weren't home to hear this mess. The last thing they needed was to come across a screaming match between me and my supposed fiancée arguing over how we weren't really engaged.

"Where are you going?" Eliza called out from behind me. The click of her heels on the tiles was the only indication she was still following me.

"I need some fresh air."

This had all been a mistake. Every last step. I never should have come here. I never should have even tried to make things better. I should have just done what any normal person would have done and let bygones be bygones. Forgotten the past, ignored it, and shoveled it down deep into the dark recesses of my soul where it would never have been heard from again.

That's what normal people did. They didn't talk about their feelings. They didn't listen to their fake fiancée or sex partner chastise them about how they were behaving like a toddler.

And I was. But who the fuck cared?

"You need to talk to someone about this." Eliza tugged on my shirt sleeve just as we crossed the threshold outside. She pulled back, stopping me long enough to move out in front of me. She held her phone out in one hand placing it between us. "If you don't want to talk to me, that's fine. But at least talk to Kinsley. It's clear there's something more going on here, and I don't want to see you ruin everything you've worked so hard for."

I took a long swig from the bottle. She wasn't making this easy. Now, she was worried about me? Did she think I was actually going to harm myself? This wasn't going to work. She was complicating things. I didn't need her caring. I didn't need to be spilling my guts out to this woman as if she were my everything.

In a couple of days, things would go back to normal. Wasn't

that what she expected? Wasn't that why she'd wanted to know when our whole arrangement would be nothing more than a thing of the past? She'd had her night of fun. In a few days, she'd have quite an impressive stack of cash for a week's worth of work. It only made sense that she'd want to cut her losses as quickly as possible, break away before anything else was expected of her.

But I wanted her around. I actually wanted things to continue on the way they were. I'd grown accustomed to someone sleeping in my bed and accustomed to her. I was accustomed to her scent, the subtle waft of cinnamon laced with jasmine that assailed me anytime she walked into a room. I would miss the sound of her laughter, her smile, and even the fucking irritated glare she poised at me now.

I would miss it all, while she couldn't wait for it to all be over.

"Fuck." The word slipped out. I took another gulp of whiskey to drown out my thoughts. Was I actually falling for this woman?

"Well? Are you going to call her?" Eliza asked.

I clenched my jaw. Maybe it was time to reestablish boundaries. Whatever the hell those were. Where did you rank someone you were sleeping with, who was also pretending to be your fiancée, but was technically in your employ? I'd let her get too close to me already. All while she was counting down the days.

"This may come as a surprise to you, Eliza, but I don't take orders from you," I said. "You're still my employee. Which means you work for me. So, you do as I say and that's final. And I'm saying to let it go."

The closest thing I'd ever come to seeing fire stream through a person's eyes was right there in that moment. She ripped the bottle from my hand and grabbed a piece of my shirt in a fist with the other. She tugged me close against her, practically down to her eye level, and forced me to hold her glare.

"Let's get one thing straight, Mr. Alexander." I never hated the sound of my name more than in that moment. "You may be my boss. You may have more money than I will ever see in my lifetime. But I am not your inferior. So, don't you ever treat me like one."

She released me and took her own swallow of whiskey before handing the bottle back to me. I'm the one who usually liked being in control, liked calling the shots and taking command when necessary. But I wasn't going to lie ...

... That was fucking hot.

Eliza walked past me toward the door.

"Where are you going?" I asked.

"Giving you what you want," she said. "Your space."

The door slammed shut, and a gnawing sense of fear for where she planned to go took hold. She could be headed to Sawyer's or to take the next flight out of town. I couldn't say I blamed her, nor had I any right to stop her. The feelings that overcame me at the possibilities bore with them a whole new level of anguish.

I didn't want her to leave, and none of the reasons had anything to do with saving face in the middle of the mess I'd created. I sure as hell didn't want her to be with Sawyer. Just the thought of her fucking another man made me want to down the remainder of the bottle in my hands.

Amidst all of these agonizing thoughts, I was struck by the

worst realization I could have ever imagined. I was not falling for Eliza after all.

Somewhere along our little charade, I'd already taken the plunge.

Chapter Fifteen

ELIZA

$\mathcal{W}$e hadn't discussed how long our engagement would last once we left Louisiana.

We'd barely even discussed the issues surrounding his childhood hangups. We were nowhere near making any headway on the most imminent problems in our supposed relationship and were even further away from closing the deal on the Montgomery Plantation.

Justin needed to get a handle on his emotions. Whatever anger and resentment he held towards his family and this town leaked into every aspect of his work, at least when it came to this property.

He was hiding something. Rosalie had been right. Family was everything. A man's history spoke volumes of his character and how he cherished the legacy of those who came before him. Justin didn't seem to care for either. It would make sense if his parents mistreated him. But they weren't even embarrassing.

Bob and Debbie were refined and loving parents. By all

appearances, they were even amazing friends and citizens. If evidence of how his mother interacted with all of her guests at the party stood to reason, she was beloved by many. Not to mention how everyone treated her when we'd gone into town for lunch earlier in the week.

While her son paid his family little attention at all.

It didn't make any sense. Why go through all this trouble to open something like this here? Justin didn't want to be here. He didn't want to visit more often once all of this was over. Otherwise, he would have answered the question Rosalie had asked without hesitation or confusion. At this point, I wasn't even sure if he knew why he wanted the property, other than it was close to family and friends he'd striven his whole adult life to be without.

Was he trying to make up for something? Did he think bringing in a whole new area of economic growth would make up for the years he was gone?

Maybe it was some other sort of grand gesture. He planned to make the place a non-profit. Even though he said he hadn't stamped out all the details for what that non-profit was meant to be, it had to be a lie. Justin always knew what he wanted. He always had a plan in mind for these types of things. He had a vision for this property, though he wasn't sharing it with the one person who stood in the way of him achieving it. Why?

I returned to the bed and breakfast later that night. Two couples had checked in for the week, so we were no longer alone with his parents in this big empty house. It also meant no more fighting. Not that I missed that.

I'd never been so angry with anyone in my entire life. It took every last ounce of compassion to return. I'd contemplated all manner of retreat, hopping on the next flight out of town or finding a hotel for the night. I didn't want to see him. Not after all the things he'd said.

Did he really believe all those things? Did he really still see me as his employee and nothing else? Was I even surprised?

Whether I'd expected it or not, it didn't ease the ache it caused. I was stupid to let him make me feel like I was anything more, like I somehow matter to him.

Because I clearly didn't.

Instead, I returned to his parents' bed and breakfast after an hour-long conversation with my sister, in which she'd finally convinced me murder was never the answer. I swapped a few stories with the two couples and his parents. All of them sat around a warm fire in the living room.

It wasn't even that cold, but it felt cozy all the same. Justin, of course, was nowhere to be seen.

When I'd finally made my way up to the room, he was passed out in a chair, the whisky bottle dangling precariously between his fingers. It was good that he didn't love me. Wonderful that he never could. Better to find out now than to fall even harder for him.

I awoke the next morning to find Justin standing over me, toothbrush in hand and wearing the pair of sweatpants I had helped him into last night. I had nearly wrestled him out of the chair, into the bed, and removed part of his clothes before he'd insisted he wasn't a child and could do it himself.

Now, he looked somewhat polished and refreshed,

completely free of a hangover despite downing an entire bottle of whiskey.

I started at the sight of him standing over me, letting out a curse or two before leaping to a sitting position.

"What the hell?" I shouted.

"I'm not a drunk," was his only response.

"What?"

"In case you thought last night was a normal thing for me. It wasn't," he explained. "I don't normally drink like that. I prefer being in control."

I tossed the covers back and pushed past him toward the bathroom. "I'm very well aware of your need for control."

"You came back," he said, filling the doorway with his large frame. Seeing the man shirtless, hair all tousled, and sporting that sheepish grin was almost enough to make me forgive him.

Almost.

"Where else was I supposed to go?" I asked.

He shrugged. "Back home. To a hotel."

A wry laugh slipped past my lips. "Trust me. The thought had crossed my mind."

I shut the door to the bathroom. I needed my privacy, not even just to get ready in the morning. Maybe Justin had been right. While not the most delicate way to handle things, we needed to reestablish boundaries.

I was his employee. I was not his fiancée. And we were never going to sleep together again.

I opened the door after thirty minutes, hoping he'd finally taken the hint and left. He sat in the chair, fully dressed and pouring over notes I'd made in his proposal form. When I entered, he looked up from the pages, and a softness overtook his features. "I'm sorry for what I said."

I cocked my head to the side. Now was not the time to fall for his charm. He may be sorry now, but what about further down the line? We would never be equals in the ways that mattered.

"It's fine," I said. "I just want to get through this day and be done with it."

"Done with what?"

"All of it." The words came out harsher than I'd intended. He seemed taken aback, completely confused by my sudden vehemence to be rid of him.

Or maybe not confused. Just disappointed.

The rest of the day carried on like that. Neither one of us knew how to respond to the other, unsure of what the other wanted to hear. Too many emotions spiraled within me, whirling like a cyclone ready to destroy all critical functions in its path. It was torture being near him, not touching him, being angry instead of wanting to reach out and nurture whatever aches he suffered.

Every instinct begged me to rescue him, to pull him out of the dark quagmire in which he was drowning. But that was the job of a girlfriend, a fiancée, or even a friend. All of which I was not, or so he'd made perfectly apparent the previous night.

Instead, I dressed for the gala when the time came and donned a lovely mask adorned with peacock feathers to match my sapphire blue gown. Justin wore a plain black tux, not that I was surprised. At least he wore what looked like a half cape and a black mask to give a more festive look to his attire.

It was the first masquerade I'd ever attended. Nothing this

fancy or extravagant had ever crossed my path growing up in the lower middle class. It was the sort of thing reserved for fairytales and movies where guests in lavish gowns walked down a cobblestone road lit with torches and lanterns. One where all the characters, whether named or background filler, approached a castle too brilliant for words.

Only in this case, the castle was the Montgomery Plantation, though it didn't take away from the majesty of our arrival. Even the exterior sported a whole new look from the previous day. Rosalie had placed out hay bales and pumpkins, some painted and some carved and illuminated with a soft, spooky glow. It all looked so magical and festive already. And we hadn't even stepped foot inside.

"Shall we?" Justin asked, holding out his arm to me.

I took it, hesitant and feeling even more like a damsel from one of those romantic books of the past. Only this time, I didn't need a hero to save me. I was more than capable of saving myself from the big, bad prince.

"Welcome, my darlings," Rosalie greeted us at the door, wearing a soft white gown with an exotic trim at the collar. Chunky gold accessories completed her attire, along with a gold mask she held away from her face on a stick. She looked like something out of an Egyptian tragedy, portraying her role with each luxurious detail.

"I'm so excited for you to finally see the interior," she said. "It's beautiful and the decorators did such a lovely job integrating the décor with the natural elements of the house. After I'm done greeting my guests, I'll come find you, Mr. Alexander. We can go over this non-profit venture you're so eager to implement in the house."

"Of course." The muscles in Justin's arm flexed. He bowed his head in agreement and led me into the ballroom.

"You still don't want to tell her what the property is going to be used for?" I asked, once out of earshot.

"It doesn't matter."

"It clearly matters to her," I said. How could he say it doesn't? "She cares about this place. She doesn't want to see it misused."

"But that's the whole point." He stopped me, turning me around to face him. "It isn't going to be misused. It'll be put to better use. To *good* use."

"Then why can't you tell her *what* it's going to be used for."

He shook his head. "Because it brings up too many other issues that I have no wish to discuss with a virtual stranger."

"You have no wish to discuss them with almost anyone," I said. This arguing was getting us nowhere.

"You ever think I don't want you knowing things for a reason?"

Here it was. This was the part where he said all this secrecy was for my protection. Was he involved in something illegal? If so, I'd already been dragged into all of this by helping with his proposals and meetings with Rosalie. I was just as far entrenched in this situation as he was, whether he wanted to admit it or not.

"And why is that?" I asked. "Too worried I might think less of you?"

Because there was no problem with that happening at this point.

He sighed, releasing his grip on my arm slowly.

"Trouble in paradise?" A voice came behind me.

The look of sheer rage on Justin's face foretold the owner

long before I turned to see him. Sawyer approached, coming to stand at my side.

"Is this man bothering you, Miss Cortez?" Sawyer asked, a sly smirk playing at his lips.

"No." I shook my head, laying a calming hand on Justin's chest and leaning in closer to him. "He was just upset about having to park the car too far away."

"Ah, I see." Sawyer chuckled. "City life making you soft, huh?"

The rapid beat of Justin's heart beneath my fingertips pulsed like a hammer struggling to break through to the other side. There were too many factors at play here with his anxiety over the property and his frustrations with me. Now, the addition of Sawyer applied a completely different role of pressure, affecting nearly all areas of his life in one fatal swoop.

Sawyer stood between him and the property, leading the way as one of the best contenders for acquiring it. At least according to Rosalie and, in not so many words, from Sawyer himself. The man also acted as a reminder of something from Justin's past he savagely longed to forget. And if the way he was holding me now was any indication, Justin hated Sawyer for a whole other reason that made just as little sense.

"I was afraid it might roll off into the swamp is all," Justin said. "Speaking of swamps, shouldn't you be getting back home?"

Sawyer grinned, genuinely amused. "Now, now. That hardly seems necessary. Especially in front of the lady."

"Yes, well, my *fiancée* and I are going to take a tour of the house," Justin said and tugged me back toward the main hallway. "If you'll excuse us."

"Allow me to show you around." Sawyer extended his arm

outward. "I've toured the estate multiple times and would be happy to oblige."

That same drumming heartbeat surged again. Only this time, Justin seemed ready to act on it. He was so close to ruining everything, falling right into Sawyer's trap and causing a scene which would oust him from the property forever. I had to do something. And there was only one thing I could think of to shift his focus.

I looped one arm around Justin's neck, placed my free hand on his cheek, and dragged him down to kiss me. Instantly, his hands wrapped around me, drawing me tighter to him. We fell into a trance more mystifying than all the wonders of the world.

When was the last time we were here? Why did it feel like all the arguments and distance placed between us slowly slipped away in an instant? Why did this feel so right, so perfect, when it was utterly wrong in so many ways?

I slipped away.

I was practically breathless by the time I turned to face Sawyer. "We would like a little privacy with our tour."

It took another hour to tour the rest of the house, only because I had to continuously convince Justin I had no intentions of repeating our little escapade in front of Sawyer.

No matter how delicious.

If anything, the kiss reminded me of how dangerous a relationship with Justin was. I needed him, body and soul. And he would simply toss me aside and shut me out whenever the mood suited him, without so much as a second thought.

How could you build on a relationship like that with someone? How could anyone with any self-worth continue on with someone without any guarantee they would love them in return? I deserved mind-blowing, super hot sex.

But I deserved to be loved even more.

"Penny for your thoughts," a voice said from behind me on the verandah.

I had stepped outside for some fresh air, while Justin discussed the details of his non-profit with Rosalie. Whether he was telling her the truth or some made up story was beyond me. But when I turned around, he was not the man standing before me.

"Haven't you caused enough trouble today?" I asked.

Sawyer grinned and moved closer to me. He leaned against the railing, staring out into the dark sky and shadowy figures of trees. The twinkle of lightning bugs flashed in and out of view like tiny green embers floating on the breeze. Everything about this place screamed beauty and peace.

So, how could such a place cause me so much pain?

"I never intended to cause trouble," he said. "Justin is just a bit temperamental."

"Can you blame him? You keep wielding your leverage over this place against him," I said. *I can't believe I'm actually defending him.* "He isn't here as much as you are, though it doesn't make the reason he wants this place any less important."

Sawyer propped himself up on one side, staring back as confused by my comment as I was. "And why does he want this place? It's not to be closer to me."

"No." I laughed wryly. "Though with such a warm welcome, I can't imagine why."

Sawyer scoffed. "Justin made his bed a long time ago."

"What does that mean?"

A menacing smile replaced the slight annoyance in Sawyer's features. My ignorance intrigued him somehow. Though if it gave me any insight into what had happened between him and Justin, I was happy to play the part. "So, he hasn't told you the story, has he?"

I shook my head.

"Well, I won't spoil the surprise, then," Sawyer said. "Tell him I did him that favor. I will say, when we all needed him here, he wasn't. Charlotte, Harrison, his parents, even me. No one could have been lower than us in that moment, and he didn't even bother to grieve with us."

"Grieve over what?"

Sawyer shook his head with a shrug. "Again, that's his territory. Not mine."

"Look, I know why you want the property," I said, which was more than I could say for Justin. "But don't you think it's time to let bygones be bygones. I've never seen him struggle so much for one property. It's clearly important to him. Can't you just back down?"

"I'm a businessman, Miss Cortez," Sawyer said, with that slow Southern drawl. Somehow it made him appear all the more charming ... and dangerous. He seemed like the devil sizing up his prey for a deal. "I don't back down so easily. Especially when the finish line is well within reach. Throw in a little revenge, and I'm even more set in my ways than before."

"So, this is all about revenge?"

"Why not?"

"Because he's trying to make amends." At least that much

was obvious. "For whatever he did, he's trying to make things right."

"Too little too late, I'm afraid," Sawyer said. "Now if you have a counter proposal, we may be able to work something out."

My eyes narrowed over him. Nothing good ever came from a deal with the devil. "Like what?"

The end of his lip twitched upward, and he shifted so he was facing the entrance back to the ballroom. "I suppose I could be persuaded by a revenge of another sort."

His eyes slid to the side, capturing mine in a stare that made my blood run cold. We were done talking. I rushed toward the exit, not even supplying an answer to his ridiculous implications. He caught me by the hand and tugged me back.

"I'm just kidding," he said, with a dry laugh. "I know he's probably told you all sorts of stories about me. It was worth it to see the look on your face."

"And if I'd have said 'yes'?" I asked.

"Then, I would have spared him from marrying a woman who quite obviously didn't take the idea of faithfulness to heart."

"Or her dignity." Maybe it had been a bluff. But if I would have agreed, he would have seized the opportunity anyway.

"That too. Either way, I'd have done him a service."

"What do you want?" I asked, yanking back on the hand he still held in his grasp.

He brought me closer, drawing the back of my hands to his lips. His mischievous eyes met mine, and he inclined his head even further. "You've already done it."

Chapter Sixteen

ELIZA

*A*ll air fled my lungs.

What the hell was he talking about? He stood close, holding me in place with some unknown force. Fear, perhaps, and a distorted curiosity to unearth the dark, twisted caverns of his mind. Yet somehow, I'd played right into his trap. Whatever it may be.

"Let go of my fiancée." Justin's voice grumbled from across the way. All at once, the scheme grew sickeningly obvious, and I played the unwitting pawn.

I jerked back, finally able to free my hands from Sawyer's overpowering grip. Heat flushed to my cheeks. I pressed a hand to my face to quell the fevered flashes and took another step away from Sawyer. It must have made me look even more guilty, though no one could deny the anger streaked across my expression.

Turns out, I really could want to murder more than one person in a week.

"I was just congratulating her on your engagement," Sawyer said, holding a hand outward in a casual gesture, as if remarking on nothing more than the weather instead of a purported innuendo. "She is quite lovely."

Justin leapt forward, but I placed myself in front of him. He stopped, inhaling one long draw of breath to calm him.

"Enough. Both of you," I said. I tugged on Justin's collar, drawing his attention down to me. The hard glare in his gray eyes softened only slightly as they captured mine. Sawyer was not the only one he was angry at, though this time I couldn't completely blame him. "You've said all you need to Rosalie, and I've had more than my fair share of deception here. So, let's just go."

I looped my arm around his and dragged him down the verandah steps. We made our way down the cobblestone drive, taking a different path from the day before, toward where the cars were parked. It was a long way to the car. Especially in heels and a dress made for ballrooms alone.

It would likely be a long car ride, too.

"Do you want to talk about what Rosalie said?" I asked.

"It's safe to say I'm not in a talking mood at the moment, Eliza," Justin explained, taking a stride ahead of me. "Though feel free to share your account of the evening. What is it? One billionaire not enough for you?"

Of all things. The man was jealous! Though I'm sure his pride being wounded played more of a hand in it than actual jealousy. It wasn't me he feared losing. It was that he was losing anything, the property or his supposed fiancée, to Sawyer.

"Of course not, sweetheart," I said coyly. "We both know Sawyer isn't worth nearly as much as you are."

He rounded on me, rapidly closing the distance between us in a matter of seconds. "You think this is funny?"

"I think it's funny. For someone who's so ready to be rid of me, you're throwing around the *F* word quite a bit today." He stared back at me, confused. "Not that one."

"No one ever said I was ready to be rid of you," he said. "And for all intents and purposes, he does think you are my fiancée, which makes his behavior all the more inappropriate."

Justin turned, walking back toward the car. We made it maybe another few steps before he turned back and added, "And you're the one who's trying to get rid of someone. Isn't that why you keep asking when all of this is going to be over?"

My jaw dropped. Actually, fucking dropped like some sideswiped cartoon character. He couldn't be serious. Was that why he was so angry? He thought I was counting down the days to being done with him.

"Because I'm tired of playing these games with you," I said. "I'm tired of being somewhere between fiancée and fucktoy."

He tipped his head to the side. This time, sincerity overtook frustration, and it was so tempting to believe whatever came out his mouth next. "It's not like that."

"Oh really?" I asked. Because it sure as hell felt like it. Wasn't I just his employee? Not his confidant or his girlfriend. I was just someone to do his bidding whenever he pleased, and I had already agreed, like an idiot, to all of it. "How much of that two hundred thousand went toward my services on Thursday? Do you think I should charge extra?"

Well, that pissed him off. "Stop it."

"Why?" I tipped one coy shoulder upward. "You made it

clear, I am nothing but your employee. So, how much do you usually charge for that sort of thing?"

He sighed and dragged a hand across his face. "I said I was sorry."

"Well, it wasn't enough."

"Then what is?"

"Tell me what happened between you all," I said, ignoring the scoff that accompanied my request. "You're so adamant about getting this property, which is literally too close to home. But you haven't told anyone why it's so important. You talk about non-profits and expanding to other properties, but you gave no indication of how this relates to the hotel industry."

Justin ran a hand against the back of his neck, either trying to concoct an impressive response or stop the beginning of a horrible headache. Maybe both. "That isn't your concern."

"Like hell it isn't. I'm just as involved in this as you are." I felt like those guys large corporations set up to take the fall for giant Ponzi schemes. I was so deep in this mess. Everyone knew my name. Everyone had a specific idea of my relationship with the man in charge. And yet, I knew absolutely nothing. I could be a part of some grand money laundering scheme and be none the wiser.

"I need to know if something illegal is going on or not," I added. "And not just to protect myself, but to help you sell this to Rosalie."

"You really think I'd do something like that?"

I held my arms out in confusion. "I'm not sure what you're capable of, Justin. Last week, I would have thought you incapable of abandoning your friends and family for a decade without so much as a word spared between you. Your mother said she only hears from you two to three times a year."

He started back toward the car with a soft laugh. "Not everyone is close with their family."

"Not everyone has a *good* family," I corrected, following after him. "And you do. Your parents care about you. They keep tabs on you through the internet just so they can respect your need for space but still make sure you're alive before they go to bed each night. You made no plans to reach out to them when you arrived, yet, the second they heard you were coming, they organized a welcome home party."

"Yes, well us Southerners will come up with any excuse to throw a party with alcohol," he called out over his shoulder, unlocking the car in front of him and sliding into the seat.

"Unbelievable." I contemplated not getting into the car. That would certainly show him. I could hail a taxi, stay the night in a hotel like I'd planned, and not see him again until our flight the next morning.

But I loathed the idea of walking all the way back to the house on this cobblestone, in these heels, and in a dress that felt like it weighed a ton.

I climbed into the seat on the passenger's side. To my surprise, he hadn't started the car. He held the keys in one hand. The other pressed firmly into the bridge of his nose.

"It's Pete," he said, barely audible. I wouldn't have even known what he'd said if I hadn't heard the name passed from one person to the other, completely meaningless every time. Or so I thought.

"Pete?"

Justin nodded. "A couple years into our service in the

marines, my buddy Pete and I were deployed to the Sangin district. It was a fucking hellhole. There were so many land mines, we could barely even move through the area."

He inhaled a steadying breath, pressing his fist gingerly against the steering wheel as if pacing his words. Already, I witnessed the ghosts resurrecting, the phantoms of the past twisting him in their grasp like rubber. I'd never seen a man so haunted. I almost regretted ever asking.

"We'd come under fire, and we couldn't even duck for cover or roll out of the way without potentially setting off an explosive," Justin continued. "We'd just have to sit there and take it."

I reached out, taking his hand in mine. He looked up at me, and I noted the first rim of red along the edges of his eyes. He forced a smile, followed by a sigh and a half-hearted laugh. His whole demeanor changed in an instant, and he straightened, despite the obvious pain his memories caused him.

"Pete's parents hadn't wanted him to join the military," he said. "But he'd wanted to go. I was supposed to look after him. I mean, what were the odds that we'd been deployed at the same time? Then ... he died. There was nothing I could do to save him."

"It wasn't your fault." How could he even take all of that on himself?

"No." He shook his head. "But when I was released, I was so ... messed up by the whole ordeal, I didn't even want to see anyone. I could barely even drive. I just ... kept feeling like I was back there. Waiting for the next device to go off."

"How long did it take?" I asked.

"I don't know." He shook his head, not even looking at me but into a world all its own. "I don't even remember. I still have nightmares every now and then. Every time I thought about coming home, I just thought about Pete. I thought about his parents and about how I'd let everyone down."

"You didn't let anyone down," I said, stroking his cheek and drawing his gaze back to mine. "You had a normal reaction to a very traumatic experience. And you're not the only one. They would understand if you just told them."

"It means opening up too many wounds." He shook his head. His hand closed around mine, bringing it down to his lips and pressing a kiss to my palm. "It's better this way. Less guilt on my part. They can hate me all they want for staying away. I deserve it. But at least the property will help."

"What is it for?"

"It's a clinic," he said, "for homeless veterans. It provides them with PTSD therapy, medical treatment, and even a place to stay. It helps them with job placement and things of that nature."

Warmth radiated across my chest. My God, the man did have a soul. A bright beautiful one I'd misjudged all this time. "Did you tell this to Rosalie?"

Justin nodded. "Tonight, I did. I knew she would just keep asking questions, which is why I avoided it at first. I didn't want to get into all of my problems. But I told her what it was for and that I wanted to open it in honor of Pete."

Tears pricked my eyelids, drawn out by more than his need to make amends and honor someone so special to him. He had revealed so much of himself to me. He trusted me with secrets he'd spared from almost every other person in his life, even those he'd held close previously. All that smug arrogance, the rudeness he conveyed the very first weeks I knew him, all of it finally made sense.

He put on such a hard shell and wanted to block everyone out. Now, he'd finally opened up—to me. It was so raw and rare, like an uncut gem.

My hands closed around his face, bringing him back to me once again. "Thank you."

"For what?" He smiled weakly.

"For telling me," I explained. "For letting me in."

"Eliza, I—"

My fingers covered his lips. Whatever apologies he felt he needed to say could wait for another argument, another time. "It's ok."

I kissed him, letting the rhythm of our desire do all the talking. Despite all the warnings and all the alarm bells going off in my mind, I needed him. I wanted him to know how deeply I cared for him, that this was no longer a charade between two desperate people.

Somewhere along the line, I'd fallen so deeply under his spell, even before knowing his past. I'd fallen even before knowing he would share it. I was lost. But there were some things worth losing yourself for.

A soft kiss of compassion and warmth quickly blazed into a reprisal for more. It had been two days since we'd been together, two days since we had even kissed, not counting the quick kiss in the hallway. I'd never needed sex before. I'd been content without it all these years. Only now that I had a taste of what it could be like, with a man who left me breathless, I refused to deny myself any longer.

I pulled back, hiking the edges of my skirt up until they

formed a bunch around my waist. I crossed over the center console and straddled his lap. It was the most awkward maneuver possible, but it didn't matter. Justin didn't seem to care, and that's all that mattered to me in that moment.

"Well, Miss Eliza," he said in his Southern drawl that he had supposedly lost after years of conditioning, though it still suited him. "I've never seen you so forward."

"I've never wanted something more," I said, pressing a kiss against his throat.

"Finally, something we can agree on." His hands moved between my thighs, reaching down for something beneath the seat. He slid the chair back even further than his long legs required. I wriggled beneath him as his touch awakened stirrings I thought I might never revisit again.

I made my way down his neck, peppering each area with kisses and slowly unbuttoning his shirt. He had tossed his tuxedo coat into the back sometime before I'd climbed into the car. There were still too many layers of clothes between us, but one less would make me feel that much closer.

I needed this. One last night before everything changed. One last night before the spell wore off, and everything went back to the way things were.

Not everything, at least. My family would finally have the money they needed to pay all those medical bills. I'd finally be able to go back to school. And one way or another, it was all thanks to Justin.

His knuckles trailed along the thin cloth separating my womanhood from his touch. I trembled, weakened to the point of almost collapsing. I was losing all concentration, all control.

But it was worth it.

"You're going to have to remove these," he said, still drawing lazy circles atop the fabric. Every stroke lit my skin like wildfire.

I needed him now. But God, this dress made it so hard to do anything. "I can hardly move in this thing."

"I have a plan," he whispered, his breath feathering across my lips in warm temptation. "But you'll have to trust me. Do you?"

I nodded, knowing my trust in him was only halfway assured. I knew he would never cause me physical harm and that he would honor any deal made between us. But I wasn't entirely sure this man before me wouldn't break my heart.

A sharp rip tore through the enclosed space of the car. The pieces of my underwear fell to the edge of each thigh, and it took me a full ten seconds to realize what he'd actually done.

"Did you just tear my underwear off?" I asked, stunned, though even more so intrigued.

He looked up at me, my hair enclosing our faces like a curtain. "It was the most practical thing to do."

"I actually liked that pair."

He brushed the hair out of my face and brought me closer. "Then I'll buy you a hundred more."

Our lips met and once again, I felt that tension surging within me like a flood. It was almost as if something might spill out over the top at any moment. I needed that connection with our bodies joined as one in the most sacred, primal of ways. I needed that feeling of fulfillment, enveloping me in ways I'd never imagined possible.

It took mere moments to unhook his belt and free his erection. He felt warm and smooth between my palms. A sensation of power overtook me, knowing that I could draw out this type of desire and that a man like Justin Alexander wanted me. He could have any woman he wanted. He certainly could have a more accommodating woman who didn't chastise him and who surrendered to his every whim.

But he wanted me. At least, for now.

I stroked my hands up along the length of him, enjoying the feel of him beneath my touch. I wasn't entirely sure what I was doing. It wasn't as if I'd had years of practice in this type of thing. There was only one way to learn, and if I was to ask anyone without feeling foolish, it was Justin.

"Show me," I said. "Show me how to please you."

He smiled, shaking his head as if confused. "You already please me."

"I want to do it better." Maybe he didn't realize how inexperienced I was. Something I honestly thought impossible. When would be the right time to tell him something like that? Would it freak him out to know that he'd been my first? "Show me."

"Whatever you wish," he said and closed his hand over mine, guiding me.

The pulsing between my thighs intensified. Watching him, eyes closed and pacing each breath, inspired a whole new string of wicked thoughts and all the things he still had left to teach me. They reminded me of all the many pleasures I'd yet to unearth.

Would it all really be over after tonight?

He stopped, pulling my hands from his hardened erection and placing his hands at my thighs. "I need you, Eliza. Right now."

I nodded, letting him pull me further up his lap. I was the one in control this time. I was the one on top, in charge of the pace and movements. Though I knew nothing beyond what instincts driven purely by desire told me to do.

The tip of his erection brushed across my entrance. Soft tremors overtook my body, succumbing to a need withheld for far too long. Justin's hand slipped over my hip, directing me forward until he finally slid inside me. I rocked against him. Streams of ecstasy shimmered through my veins. Every question and every fear faded away until only he remained.

His hands gripped my thighs, coaxing me upward, forward. Each movement made me radiate from the inside out. I'd never felt so complete. All my life I'd kept my head down, distancing myself from the possibility of connecting with anyone. It never seemed as important as family, my career, and an inherent need to navigate the emotional waters of grief and survival. Only now, I feared I needed Justin the same way I needed all of those things and more.

Life would never be the same without him.

The tension inside me pulled tighter, drawing at all sides until they scattered in sparkling waves of starlight. I let out a cry of pure bliss as I crumbled against his shoulder.

His grip on my thighs tightened, and he thrust into me again. Just a few quick strokes sent me soaring back over the edge into that wonderful feeling somewhere between madness and magic. That second spell of ecstasy poured over me in a warm, golden rush of sunshine, faster and more intense than the first. I felt practically numb by the time he came, and we crashed in a fit of trembling breaths.

We sat in silence. My face pressed against his shoulder. He smelled of spiced musk and sandalwood. His arms around me felt like home, and there was nothing more perfect in that moment than being wrapped in his embrace. I was in even bigger trouble than I'd thought. I didn't want all of this to end. I didn't want to pretend he no longer meant the world to me.

Tomorrow would determine where he stood on our relationship. It would determine whether he still saw it as another business transaction or something more. Maybe, he wouldn't want to set an end date. Maybe he would say how deeply he needed me in return.

Or he would confirm my worst suspicions that I had fallen so desperately in love with a man who could never feel the same for me in return.

Chapter Seventeen

JUSTIN

"Are you ready?"

I gripped Eliza by the arm and drew her gaze to meet mine. She was stiff all over again, staring at the boarding dock like the entrance to Hell.

She nodded weakly. "I can do this."

"Yes, you can," I said and stroked her back tenderly. "It's just a quick flight to New Orleans, then we connect to San Francisco. Piece of cake."

She refused to take anything to calm her nerves. Not even a glass of alcohol to make conquering one of her greatest fears more palatable. I would find some way to distract her, something to keep her mind off of things. The way I had before.

Maybe not exactly the same way I had before. Though she did seem to ease whenever she talked about her family. She'd spent a whole week without them, stealing away to answer phone calls whenever she could and dodging questions about her engagement.

What had she told her parents? Did they all know it was one giant charade? What would they think of their daughter being engaged to a billionaire?

For real.

Now that was crazy talk. What the hell was coming over me? I wasn't a family man. That much came clear during this last visit home. The last thing I wanted to do was be surrounded by people with too many expectations who sought only to find the good in me even when I brought them nothing but disappointment.

There was little good left in me—not anymore.

Even with this new venture, I could not consider myself a whole new man. The clinic in Louisiana was only one of many I'd been collecting throughout the years. It was just the final icing on the cake—the last piece of the puzzle to make my network of reparations complete. All across the country, we would open clinics in Pete's name with the home base located right there in the sleepy little town he grew up in.

Still, it only made up for the sins of my past which did not include all the ones I intended to make in the future, and there would be plenty.

"Is your family happy to have you home?" I asked, once we were finally seated.

"Yes." She nodded, visibly shaking. "My mom said my dad's treatment is coming along well. And my sister has been staying over to help around the house."

"What have they said about the engagement?"

She shrugged. "Gabi said there were a couple of reporters outside the day of the actual announcement. But after that, they've only had the random person or two poking around and asking them questions. My mother is not very happy about it, but they are managing."

"Have you told them ..."

"That it's not real?" An amused scoff blew past her lips. "No, I just told them I would explain more about it when I came home."

"And what do you plan on telling them?" I asked.

"The truth." She cast a flippant gesture through the air. "Most of it, at least. It was all a misunderstanding, but we had to keep up appearances to help seal the Montgomery deal. I'll tell them something along those lines."

She closed her eyes and pressed her head back against the seat. The engines whirred to life, and I took her hand in mine. She gently squeezed as the plane started to move, holding on to me for dear life it seemed.

Eliza was no different from all the others I'd left in Louisiana. She wanted to only see the good. And good God, she made me want to give it to her. I had almost come close to telling her I loved her last night in the car. Though she'd stopped me before I could make a fool out of myself.

Did I love her? I cared about her more than anyone else in this world. The last thing I wanted to do was disappoint or hurt her like she said I would.

Even looking at her now, riddled with fear and finding comfort only in my touch, made me realize how badly I wanted to protect her. I wanted to always be the one to calm her fears, to comfort her, and to shield her from the world and assholes like Sawyer. Just the thought of her with someone else drove me to the breaking point. If I let her go, I risked much more than no longer calling her mine.

She could marry someone else. Not right away but eventually. I never cared about my other partners finding their perfect match. But with Eliza, it might damn near kill me.

"Maybe we should talk about time frames," I said.

Her eyes flicked open. "Like, when this is going to be over?"

A lump formed in the base of my throat making it difficult for me to swallow or even move. Somehow, I still managed a tight nod.

"Fine," she said. "What did you have in mind?"

"I don't know. It really just depends on what your plans are."

"My plans?"

"Yes. I mean, there will be a lot involved when we get back." Maybe she didn't realize how much would change. We'd been living in a bubble for the past week. Now, we would be forced to deal with what being together might really be like. Would she fit into my life the way I wanted her to? Would she even want any part of it at all when she had a family of her own to worry about?

"You'll be expected to go with me to company events," I explained. "We'll need to be seen out in public together."

She cast me a sideways glance, withholding none of her disgust at the idea. "Like on a date?"

"Is that so bad?"

She softened and shook her head. "No, I just ... isn't that going to be awkward with work?"

Work? God, what the hell were we going to do about work? I had every intention of keeping her on for the next couple of weeks while Kinsley found a replacement. Truth be told, she'd already been in the process of looking and could be vetting my new assistant as we spoke. With all the money she was getting, Eliza had plenty of time to decide how she wanted to handle the situation. She didn't need to work for a little while, at least. Though I had no idea how deep in debt her family truly was either.

"Do you still want to work?" I asked.

"Won't you still need an assistant?"

I ground my teeth. This was getting us nowhere. Why couldn't she just say what she wanted? "That wasn't what I asked."

"Well, I can't take off work indefinitely," she said, subtle notes of anger and irritation seeping through. Great, now I'd pissed her off. "I may as well be of use in the meantime."

"I thought you wanted to move up and go back to school."

"I do." She stared off into the seat cushion in front of her, as if it harbored all the secrets of the universe between its threads. "Though I'm not entirely sure when that will be possible."

"Damn it, Eliza." My fingers pressed against my forehead, smoothing the wrinkles slowly forming there. "What do you want? Just say it and it's yours. If you want to work, fine. You can stay my assistant and apprentice with me until you go back to school."

"But what will people say?" she asked.

"Who cares what they say? The story states that you were already my girlfriend before you came to work for me. You came in as a favor to me, then decided you liked it."

"People will think—"

"I'm not giving you any power," I explained. "I'm giving you experience. You're free to apply that experience anywhere you please once this is all over."

Her gaze drifted down to our hands, still locked together despite the many heated gestures passed between us. "And when is it over?"

We needed a set time. There was nothing more apparent in this moment than that. Unless I planned on proposing to her for real in the next couple of hours, I owed it to the both of us to end this. She didn't deserve to be strung along. She deserved the white picket fence and the happy life with a man who loved her without bounds. Someone who wouldn't disappoint her. Someone who hadn't roped her into some ridiculous engagement scheme that left both parties worse off than they were before.

We needed to see when this would end, no matter how painful. Because, whether we liked it or not, this would end.

"Four weeks," I said, not knowing where the number came from. "That should be enough time for me to hear back from Rosalie and to thoroughly convince everyone we were engaged before we get into things like deposits. It'll also give you enough time to figure out what you want to do, yes?"

She nodded. "In four weeks, I can either figure out something with school or get a new job."

"Perfect." I leaned back against my chair. My thumb absently stroked the back of her hand. "I'll wire the money to your account on Friday. It'll take some time to go through since your bank will probably hold it first."

"That's fine." Her eyelids squeezed tightly together. She looked almost in pain. Her fingers wriggled free of mine, and she pressed them into her temple. "I just, I think the stress of flying is finally getting to me."

"Do you need me to get you anything?"

"No." She tugged the pillow at her side free and laid it against the window. "I'm going to take a nap until we land again."

This was all for the best, wasn't it? I was not the kind of man to make someone like Eliza happy. Family meant everything to her, and I was the least likely to hold on to any lasting relationship, whether familial or otherwise.

Four weeks would be enough time to get whatever remnants of desire existed out of our system. Just like any relationship, the glitter and romance would fade with time. There was no guarantee we'd even still like each other by the end of our four weeks. We'd started off our relationship practically at each other's throats for the first week or two.

Even so, I would miss our fights. I would miss seeing all that fire and willfulness transformed into passionate hunger. In my weakest moments, I might even recall the looks of pure sympathy in her eyes. The ones that told me I wasn't a complete monster. The one that made me want to show a different side of myself to the world all over again.

But I had missed people in the past. I'd missed my family those first few years, though my guilt and drive to stay away overpowered that.

I had missed Pete. Hell, I obviously still did to some extent. Divine providence took care to ensure there was no way of getting around that. It was just something that stuck with you, like a badge of honor. Something you wore with pride despite the many ghosts surrounding its origin.

Being without the people you cared about was just another

day in the life of billionaire Justin Alexander, soulless hotel mogul and ruthless negotiator.

In four weeks, these moments would be a thing of the past. We would go back to the lives we were meant to live, separate from one another.

Four weeks and Eliza Cortez would be gone from my life forever.

Chapter Eighteen

ELIZA

hen a man asks you to pretend to be his fiancée, you realize it involves certain complications. The potential of getting too close, of falling for the lie, are all very dangerous possibilities. So why I thought I'd feel any different nearing the end of our four weeks together was beyond me.

Instead, I felt sick. So incredibly ill, in fact, it was a reasonable cause for concern.

"When does Justin get back from his business trip?" Gabi asked.

We'd been folding clothes in silence for so long, I'd almost forgotten she was here.

"Two days," I said, and straightened the tower of towels forming on the washer.

Even after I'd returned from our trip to Louisiana, Gabi had stayed home from school whenever she could. Maybe she felt sorry leaving me with the bulk of the household work. Slipping back into a normal routine while still maintaining the lie of my engagement had been anything but easy. Now, on top of two jobs, cleaning the home, cooking, and tending to my father on my mother's workdays, I had events and fake dates to deal with, too.

Justin had offered to hire someone to help. I'd promptly declined. It just didn't feel right letting a complete stranger take care of my father when I was perfectly capable of doing it myself. All it cost me was a few sleepless nights and a renewed addiction to caffeine. Although lately, I hadn't even been able to keep that down.

This whirlwind of a ride was coming to a close, at least. One week left to pretend, and it would all be over.

So why didn't that make me feel better?

"Are you ready for all of this to end?" Gabi asked.

Was I? I should be overjoyed at the thought of having my life, having a better life. "I'm ready for things to go back to normal."

"Without Justin?"

"Yes, without him," I said, not particularly caring for the implications in her tone. Did she think I was that weak? I never needed a man before. I wouldn't need one now. "That was the plan."

"You don't think the plan has changed by now?"

I slammed the sweater in my hands down onto the washer. "No, Gabi. Why would it?"

"Come on, Eliza. I've seen the way he looks at you. I've seen how you are around him. You two are absolutely crazy about each other."

I clenched my jaw, trying to drown out her deluded pleas.

She only saw part of the relationship, the one built on smoke and mirrors.

Despite our deal to maintain this charade, it had really started to feel like a relationship. We would have quiet nights at home and stolen moments at the office. He would send me flowers when no one was around to see them and check in on me on days we spent apart. He even helped me cook dinner a few nights and helped with chores when I told him we couldn't meet.

That's right. The billionaire businessman who had his own maid and personal chef on hand, actually cooked and cleaned like a commoner.

No wonder I had slowly started to believe the lie. Or why anyone else might, too. Who wouldn't be convinced with a man so masterful at his craft as Justin Alexander?

But that's all it was, a lie.

He hadn't waited even ten minutes after boarding the plane to set an end date for our relationship. I was just another negotiation, another purchase he sought to get as much use out of as possible.

And yet, every time he'd asked, I'd let him into my bed, into my home, and my heart. I knew all of this was no more than a cruel game. Yet, I still allowed myself to be taken in by the fairy-tale—the sweet, romantic ones with a happy ending—not the dark, twisted tales of suffering that warned children and adults alike that nothing was ever what it seemed, and even the kindest of strangers should never be trusted.

I was in way over my head. The sooner the fairytale ended, the sooner I could move on with my life.

"If these past three weeks have shown me anything, it's that we are most definitely not meant to be together," I said. Especially not after his ex-girlfriend cornered me at the last meeting and reminded me why I didn't belong in their world. What had she called it? *Slumming it?*

"So what?" Gabi flipped an errant gesture into the air. "One stupid woman, who is obviously jealous, says something, and you're willing to throw it all away?"

"We had a deal," I explained. "He has no intention of settling down for good. He's not the type to establish roots and start a family. These are all the things I want and everything he clearly couldn't care less about."

"Have you talked about it?"

We didn't need to talk about it. I'd seen it with my own two eyes. The man didn't care one whit about whether or not he saw his family again. The whole trip to Louisiana was a way for him to wash his hands of them for good. He would convert the Montgomery Plantation into a clinic, rid himself of any guilt, and never look back.

"Trust me," I said. "I know how he feels about family."

"Not that. Have you talked about not ending things so soon?"

Right. Because that made total sense. Let's just live in this lie even longer and make everything even more complicated than it needed to be. As if I wasn't already drowning in feelings I had no business exploring with a man who was wrong for me in so many ways.

The sex didn't make matters any less confusing. Every time we were together felt like magic and myth all rolled into one. We were both consenting adults. There was nothing wrong with enjoying ourselves and taking what we needed in that respect. I finally felt comfortable asking for what I wanted. I finally *knew* what I wanted.

And dear God, what I wanted was Justin.

"When?" I asked, my words so broken and defeated I barely recognized them. "When was I supposed to talk to him about it?"

Gabi's hand brushed my shoulder gently. "You've had three weeks. You'll have another five days by the time he gets back."

What a mess I'd gotten myself into. How was I supposed to come back from something like this?

Gabi gripped me by the arms and turned me to face her. "It's not like the two of you can go a day without talking to one another. Some fake fiancée. He goes away on a business trip for four days, and neither one of you sees it as an opportunity to drop the act."

"I'm still his assistant," I explained. There were still important business dealings to discuss, things only I could handle on my end while he was away.

"So, when he calls you every night, that's to discuss work?" Gabi asked. "Because there sure is a lot of giggling going on for talk about buying buildings and balancing budgets."

"I do not giggle."

"No, you do this weird little laugh that's kind of cute, kind of awkward," Gabi said. "But whatever. He still calls, so he obviously doesn't think it's too weird."

I gasped in a mix of shock and horror and tossed one of the unfolded shirts at Gabi's face. She dragged the piece of cloth away, laughing loudly, wickedly. For the first time since our conversation started, I felt the corner of my lips tug upward.

"All I'm saying is, you don't have to stay engaged," Gabi explained. "You can still be together though. You can still date."

I shook my head. "It would be too awkward. We're going to break our engagement but continue seeing one another. What would that look like?"

"Who says you need to break your engagement right now?"

"We can't keep prolonging this forever." I practically shouted the statement. I had been holding on to it for so long, telling myself those exact same words over and over again, that they finally broke free in a frenzy. "One month, one year. It doesn't matter. It's going to end. So, it's better to end it now before real feelings form."

My pulse raced wildly through my veins. Every part of my body burned with an intense fire. I felt as if I might combust without a moment's notice and just turn into a pile of ashy remains right there on the laundry room floor.

"Oh, *nena*." Gabi pushed back a long strand of hair covering my face. I faced her, despite not wanting to see the pity in those eyes. "Real feelings have already formed. You've spent two days without him, and you're moping around the house like a lost puppy. That's a normal weekend. What are you going to do with a lifetime without him?"

The words crashed against my chest like a blast of icy water. If the fear of collapsing on the spot no longer worried me, the threat of losing all breath would. I was two seconds from becoming a weeping mess on the floor unless I got these emotions under control.

What's wrong with me? I never would have cried over a man in the past. I never would have even put myself in a situation to feel so deeply for anyone I couldn't have. I'd known from the start that this wasn't meant to last, and yet I'd driven headlong into the heart of it. Whether I wanted to admit it or not, a lifetime without Justin was coming.

And a lifetime without him was what I would endure.

"I'll be fine," I said. "I'm fine now. It's just like sleeping without a blanket."

Gabi tipped her head to the side. Her dark eyes squinted back at me as if I'd just asked the riddle of the Sphinx. "Okay ...?"

"Like, you're just so used to having something around," I explained. "It's comforting, safe. You feel secure with it, but it isn't necessary. And after a little while, I won't need it all. Or I'll find a different blanket to wrap myself up in."

A nice warm blanket who made me feel all cozy and loved inside. The thought of another man touching me the way Justin did, holding me, made me sick to my stomach all over again.

"And what if the next blanket is a scratchy wool blanket?" Gabi asked, "or one of those thin ones they put in cheap hotels that leave you freezing all night?"

I cast her a sharp glare. "Can we just stop with the whole blanket metaphor?"

"You're the one who brought it up."

"Yeah, well, I'm starting to regret it." I loaded the last few articles of clothing into the basket, before hiking it up onto my hip and heading down the hall to my room. "Look, I'll be fine. It's better for me to nurture a heartache now rather than a year invested into something that would never work."

"Why wouldn't it work?" Gabi followed close behind me carrying her own basket of clothes to sort through.

"We don't want the same things," I said and set the basket

down on the bed. All this talk of family and relationships was making me nauseous. How much longer would I have to stomach this?

"And what do you want?" she asked.

"I ..." There was that feeling again. That same one I'd been avoiding since this morning, since yesterday. The twisting in my stomach wrenched even tighter, like knives digging in deeper. "I'm going to be sick."

I ran toward the bathroom connecting my room to the next one over. I made it with only seconds to spare before everything I'd eaten that afternoon came back up again.

"Oh my God. Are you okay?" Gabi called out behind me. "Did you eat something bad?"

It didn't stop. This was like something out of the sixth circle of Hell. Torture for all the misdeeds I'd done in the past few weeks and all the lies I had told for the sake of maintaining appearances.

Slowly, the nausea subsided. I pressed my face against the cool tiles of the bathroom walls, and let the feeling drag me back to earth. I couldn't handle much more of this. I never got sick. I had an iron stomach to match my will for all these years. Yet, my nerves must finally be getting the better of me. A person could only handle so much unease and anxiety for so long.

"Eliza?" Gabi's voice drew me back to her. "Are you okay?"

"Yeah," I said, a little dazed. She extended her hand down to me and helped me to my feet. "I've just felt sick for the past couple of days?"

"Have you been throwing up like this?" she asked.

"Only a couple of times."

"A couple times?" she said, not believing me as well as I'd hoped. "How many?"

"I don't know, Gabi." I moved to the sink and splashed my face with another cool burst of water. "It wasn't like I was keeping track."

"This is serious," she said. "What did you eat?"

I held my hand out in questioning. "Over the last few days? It's not like I've been keeping a log of that kind of thing."

"I've never seen you like this before. You're clearly sick. You should go to the doctor." The sheer horror in my sister's expression was almost enough to make me comply.

"Why?" I shrugged and made my way back to the clothes on the bed after washing up. "He'll just tell me to drink plenty of fluids, rest, and then charge me a ridiculous rate for something I could have Googled myself."

"You shouldn't be sick like this for several days."

"I didn't say several days. I said *a couple* of days."

Silence floated between us. I resumed removing the clothes from the basket and placing them back in their respective homes. Gabi simply stared at me, a curious blend of shock and pity forming amidst her soft features.

"And what if you're not sick?" she asked.

The emotions in her gaze intensified as the epiphany she had been nursing finally hit its head.

"What is that look?" I asked.

"What if you're ...you know?" Her gaze drifted down to my torso.

"What?" I bent down to capture her attention once again. "Going to sprout antennae?"

"No." She claimed a few steps between us. "What if you're going to sprout a baby?"

Dread shivered through me like the cool fingers of death. A web of ice wove its way around my throat, suffocating me until words failed to form. It would be a nightmare, an absolute nightmare to be sure. I could barely afford to take care of my family, let alone a baby. Even if his father was a billionaire, he would never want anything to do with it. He'd made it clear on more than one occasion that family was simply not his forte.

I would have the money Justin wired into my account, at least. Though that was supposed to be used on things like medical bills and paying my tuition.

Oh God. What about school? How the Hell was I supposed to do all of this, go to school, *and* take care of a baby?

My heart pounded faster, beating so intensely I pressed my hand against my chest to keep it from bursting outward. I wasn't pregnant. That would simply be that. I wouldn't worry about something I didn't need to worry about until the time came.

Meanwhile, Gabi still stood gaping at me, awaiting an answer I didn't have.

"Babies don't sprout," was all I could manage.

"You know what I mean," she said. "What if you're pregnant?"

I looked over my shoulder. The last thing I needed was for my parents to hear about this. "Keep your voice down. If Papi heard you, I would never hear the end of it."

"C'mon." Gabi cocked her head to the side and flashed one of her charming grins. "He'd love a little grandbaby."

"Not out of wedlock." God, I sounded like some hopeless damsel in a period drama. It didn't change the fact that my family would think of this as an overall bad thing, no matter how much they would love any child once it was born. "Mama would kill me. And I'm not pregnant."

"This isn't the Stone Age, Eliza."

"Tell that to them." I needed to find something to keep myself busy. I put the rest of the clothes away. There was only one way to settle this—a pregnancy test. If that came back positive, then I could come up with a plan from there. Until then, there would be no need to worry.

But if it did come back positive ... what then?

"Were you safe?" Gabi asked.

"I'm on birth control." That's right. I am on birth control. I even had my period a week ago. A sigh of relief pulsed through me. I wouldn't be experiencing morning sickness that quickly, would I? And even though birth control had its limits, it was still highly effective, wasn't it?

Gabi stared down her nose at me, still awaiting my response. "That's not what I asked."

"We may not have always been as careful as we should have," I said.

"*Babosa!* Are you serious?"

"No need for name-calling," I said. "I thought we didn't live in the Stone Age."

"We don't. That's why you should know better."

I sighed. This was getting us nowhere. "It's not like we don't know each other. I wasn't particularly worried about his history, and he has nothing to worry about with me."

"But now you're pregnant."

"We don't know that!"

"Then, I'll pick up a test today, and you're taking it," Gabi said.

I didn't want to do this. And why? Because the thought had already crossed my mind so many times that I couldn't even count all the conversations I had with myself. I'd discounted the possibility every time.

But it had crossed my mind for a reason.

Something wasn't right. Whether I wanted to admit it or not, I needed to at least rid myself of this as a possibility altogether.

I nodded. "Fine. Bring it here tonight, and we'll know for sure."

Chapter Nineteen

JUSTIN

The first thought to cross my mind when the plane landed was to see Eliza.

It had been four days without her in my bed and four days without holding her in my arms, seeing her smile, and breathing in her intoxicating scent.

All of it would be over in five days if I didn't do something about it. Letting the engagement go a little longer wouldn't hurt. Maybe it would be better if we let things fall apart organically. We could fall out of love, or lust, or whatever this was, rather than deny ourselves something we truly wanted.

I wasn't the only one who would appreciate this. Eliza wanted things to stay the same. I could feel it. She just needed me to start the conversation. I needed to speak my peace first, so she felt confident enough to voice what she wanted.

Right. When had Eliza ever had a problem voicing what she wanted? She knew exactly what she wanted and how to ask for it. And I was foolish enough to comply, no matter what the costs

—even if it meant losing my heart to a woman who would cut me loose in mere days without a second thought.

An eternity without her seemed too harsh a sentence to bear, even for someone like me who deserved all the misery in the world.

"It took you long enough." A voice came from my side. I turned to find Kinsley standing beside me in the middle of airport arrivals.

"What are you doing here?" I asked.

She motioned toward an exit and led me out to our private car. "I thought you could use a friendly face on the drive back home."

"Then you should have sent my fiancée." The subtle notes of disappointment irked me more than the actual disappointment. Why hadn't Eliza come to the airport? And why the hell did it matter so much to me?

"She's back at the office, holding down the fort," Kinsley said. "She's actually quite good at it, you know."

The car doors slammed closed. She directed the driver to head back to the office, then raised the glass partition separating the driver from us.

"One more thing ..." Kinsley tapped a curious finger to her chin. "You know she's not really your fiancée, right?"

Silence was the only answer to her question I could offer.

"Or is she?"

"Kinsley ..." I growled.

"I mean, how long are you going to carry on like this?" she asked, her hand gestures growing more volatile with each word. "I watch the two of you, and it's like watching a train collision in slow motion."

"Thanks."

Kinsley leveled her eyes over me. "All I'm saying is, you know the end is coming. She knows it's coming. Yet, it's clear to everyone with eyes that it's the last thing you both want. It's a disaster waiting to happen. I keep yelling out warnings, but it means absolutely nothing to either of you. You're both going to destroy one another needlessly, and I'll be the one who has to clean up the mess."

"While I appreciate your concern, it's not necessary." If and when I decided to renegotiate the terms of my agreement with Eliza, it would be because I was certain it was what we both wanted. While everyone else may see a happy couple, it was precisely because we'd orchestrated things to look that way.

You're a fucking idiot.

Of course, I was. I was happy for the first time in my life because of Eliza, not because of the lie. She made me feel whole in all the ways my career never had. I'd been running from my family and my past for so long, I'd forgotten to run toward something, instead. I'd always thought my career fulfilled me. Each new acquisition, every other million to line my bank account, and the many women throwing themselves at my feet should have made me feel proud, accomplished, and powerful —successful.

None of it made me feel the way Eliza did. And now, I was to be hanged by a noose of my own making. I thought putting a time limit on things made it easier for the both of us to walk away. Only now, it felt more like a ticking time bomb waiting to explode.

"So, you're going to propose to her for real, then?" Kinsley asked.

My brows knit together, and I pinned her with a stone-cold glare. "How did we go from destroying one another to proposing?"

"If you end your engagement to one another, you'll both end up hurt."

I sighed. Dammit, if she wasn't right. "I know."

"So, what are you going to do about it?"

"I don't know, Kinsley." The words tumbled out in a boom that echoed through the small car. For all Kinsley's worth, she simply sat there staring, completely unnerved by my sudden outburst. I drew in one pacing breath before adding, "I haven't thought that far ahead. I don't want to lose her, but that doesn't mean I want to get married."

"You want to keep your options open." Kinsley nodded and peered out the window. "I get it."

"What? No." *God, no!* For once, another woman was the furthest thing from my mind. "I don't ... *need* anyone else. I don't even want to think about what my life will be like without her."

"Well, just fast-forward to Sunday."

"Stop," I grumbled.

"I'm being honest with you," Kinsley said. "Can you say the same for yourself?"

I propped my chin against my fist and peered out the window to clear my thoughts. Though I didn't want to hear it, Kinsley was right. If I didn't do something about this soon, the world I troubled over imagining would become reality.

"You love her," she whispered, seemingly arriving at her conclusion for the first time despite all her chastisements.

My eyes flicked upward, capturing her distressed gaze with my own. "I'm very well aware."

Her demeanor shifted. She nearly bounced upward in a mix of pure joy and annoyance. "Then what is the problem?"

I shrugged. How the hell was I supposed to answer that? I wasn't ready. I wasn't even a hundred percent sure this was how far I wanted to take things. Just because you loved someone didn't mean you automatically spent an eternity with them. Love didn't always last. Sometimes, it just happened.

It never happened before.

"I don't even know how to be a husband," I said, unable to think of a better excuse.

"Well, that's stupid," Kinsley replied. "Who does, other than, like, second or third husbands? And even then, they've screwed up a few times, too."

"Is this supposed to help?"

"Yes, because you need some tough love right now," she said. "Stop being a baby, and just tell her how you feel. Take things from there. Some engagements last years."

The car pulled to a stop, and the doorman for our building helped Kinsley out of the car. Eliza was a few short steps and one quick elevator ride away. It would take a matter of minutes before she was in my arms again, and it was all I could do not to run.

A flurry of emotions stirred within my chest. Was I really this excited to see her again? Maybe, it was just the anxiousness surrounding our next conversation. There was no guarantee she would want to keep things as they were. There was an even more unlikely chance she'd consider the possibility of a real engagement.

Each ding on the elevator instilled its own brand of precious torture. I was literally counting down the floors, shifting between feelings of pure terror and pure bliss. The doors slid open, and in an instant, all doubt faded.

Eliza sat at her desk, eyes fixed to the computer screen and tapping a pen against her lips in meditative thought. I never thought I could be so jealous of a fucking pen, and yet here I was. The raucous thundering of my heartbeat stilled. My pounding pulse ebbed to nothingness as I stood completely paralyzed.

Fuck! I'm in so much trouble.

When she looked up at me, her gold eyes glittered with all the brilliance of unearthed treasure. Forgetting all pretense and all the doubts swirling about my head, I bent down and scooped her up into my arms. My name breezed across her lips just before I took them with my own, claiming her after what felt like an eternity apart.

She melted against me. Her arms encircled my neck, and she dropped whatever inhibitions dissuaded her from giving in at first. What did it matter if the whole office stared? To them, we were truly engaged, deeply in love, and unable to stand another moment apart. To them, it made sense I would want to kiss my fiancée the moment I walked through the door.

These feelings made sense to everyone but me it seemed. I am the man who was still contemplating whether to end a fake engagement or not, saying goodbye to the woman I loved forever when I couldn't even go four days without missing her.

"Justin." Eliza pulled back, her lips still a thin distance away. "They're watching us."

"Let them watch." I shrugged and leaned in closer. "Did you miss me?"

She nodded and bit her lower lip to hide her broadening smile.

"How much?" I asked.

Her cheeks reddened, then paled all in an instant. Like someone flipped a switch and her blood fled in the opposite direction. She turned her head to the side, jaw tight and swallowing back words that failed to form.

"More than I should," she said finally, though there was little humor in them.

Did she still think this was all a game? Did she honestly think we were still putting on a show for anyone watching?

I pressed a kiss against her temple and whispered against her ear. "We have a few things to discuss."

I loosened my grip, trailing my touch down her arm until I caught her hand. Kinsley stared at the two of us, a knowing grin plastered across her face like a jester in a king's court. "Hold my calls for a while, please."

"Yes, sir." She saluted with that smug little smile, as Eliza and I disappeared behind my office door.

"They're going to think we're coming in here to have sex," Eliza said as soon as I shut the door.

I locked the door behind me, flashing her a mischievous look. "Then let's not disappoint them."

"Justin ..."

"I'm kidding." I wasn't. But there were still a few too many things to discuss first. I opened my mouth to speak and nothing spilled forth.

Dammit! Where do I even start?

"Eliza, I ..." *Love you. I can't stand the thought of losing you in just a few days. Say something, you idiot!*

There were about fifty different ways I could have said it, a hundred different intimate details I could have confessed, and yet none of them crossed my lips. All that emerged was a series of vowels and "uhs" that would have pissed off my speech teacher and got me thrown out of any legitimate meeting.

Why the hell couldn't I just say it?

You need more time. Tell her you need more time together.

"We need to talk about the money that you wired over," she said, likely seeing her only opportunity to end my stammering.

"What about it?" I asked.

Ah. So, you can talk, asshole. Fucking brilliant. We were back to talking business, when it was the furthest thing I wanted.

"It's not the right amount," she said.

I stilled. She wasn't supposed to notice. *Right.* How the hell was she not supposed to notice? In the least, she just wasn't supposed to question it. "Do you need more?"

She inched closer. A bright red blush rose in her olive cheeks —not the look of embarrassment, but one that whispered my days might in fact be numbered. It surprised me that in all the tough negotiations I'd managed throughout the years, and all the shit I'd seen in the past, this five-foot-four woman scared the hell out of me.

"You know I don't," she said through her teeth. "That's not the amount we agreed on."

"I don't understand. What's the problem?"

"It's too much. It makes me wonder what exactly the extra is for."

I froze. Now, that was hitting below the belt. "Not that."

"Then what?" she asked. "Maybe you need a little extra assurance for me to leave without looking back."

"God, Eliza. That's not why I gave you all of that." This was not how I saw our conversation going.

"It's half a million dollars, Justin. It's over twice as much as what we decided."

I shrugged indifferently. "It's really a drop in the bucket if you think about it."

"Is that supposed to make me feel better?"

"What do you want to hear?" This argument was getting us nowhere—definitely further from the conversation I did want to have. "I wanted to help in whatever way I could. I didn't want you to feel like you had to stay here. This way you can take care of your parents, go back to school, and do all the things you want to do, without worrying for a while."

She sank slowly into one of the office chairs. The agitated expression on her face morphed to a distant, lost stare into a world I could not follow. I moved in front of her, leaning against the desk as the weight of my words played across her thoughts.

"So ... you think I should leave?" she asked.

"That's not what I said." I was really fucking this up. "I just want you to have the option."

Again came that dazed expression, falling somewhere between pain and relief. She peered down at her hands, wrenching them together as if doing so might spill secrets about the future. Did she expect me to fight for her? To demand she stay with me? It was the last thing she would have wanted.

No one ever told Eliza what to do.

I still hadn't even told her how I felt. Would it even make a difference at this point?

She jerked her head upward, almost as if suddenly remembering I was still in the room. "What did you want to say to me?"

You want to tell. Here's your chance.

I reached down and pulled her to her feet. My fingertips traced her jawline, landing lightly across her lips. Her mouth parted on a quiet gasp. The dangerous rhythm of my pulse signaled one last warning before all was lost. But it was no use. I was never lost with Eliza.

I was home.

"I missed you," I said, softly. "I don't want to feel that way again."

She swallowed tightly and averted her gaze. "We only have five more days."

"It doesn't have to be."

"You're making this harder than it needs to be." Her hand flew out to my chest. She pushed back, only half-heartedly keeping me at a distance. "We had a deal. Is that what the extra money is for?"

"No. I just ..." A pang stabbed through my stomach. It nearly knocked all the air from my body. She wasn't worried the extra money was meant to make her stay. She was worried I was asking her to stay at all. "Dammit, Eliza. Are you saying you don't want this anymore?"

Her eyes slid shut. "I don't want to keep living a lie. We both deserve to follow our own paths."

"And what if all I want is you?" I asked.

The hard shell closing her off from me cracked, and she wavered as if she might crumble into pieces. For a second, I thought she might reconsider. Yet, as quickly as her vulnerability appeared, it just as swiftly vanished behind a renewed certainty.

"You can't have me," she said. "Not the way you want. It isn't fair to either of us."

I couldn't wrap my head around any of this. Here I was trying to make something real out of our relationship, and all she could do was say how much she needed the lie to be over.

It wasn't a lie, not entirely. Not on my part, at least. Maybe, I would have proposed further down the line, but she was right. There was no guarantee and no reason to prolong something that might only end in heartache.

Then, why did I already feel so awful? As if I'd been dropped to the ground by a kick to the gut.

"Until Saturday," I said, my lips at her ear. "You're still mine."

She nodded. "Yes."

My lips found the sensitive space behind her ears. I relished the sound of her sudden intake of breath, the one that told me far more than words. "And it's been four days since I've touched you."

Each breath she took rose like a gasp for air. The hand at my chest curled into a fist around my shirt, drawing me closer instead of further away. Impulsively, I looped my arm around her waist and spun her back to sit atop my desk. Her eye level practically matched mine for once.

I positioned myself between her thighs, letting my hands follow the path of her rising skirt until I felt the lace fringe on her underwear. She shuddered and the muscles in her legs weakened with desire.

I brushed my lips against hers. "I'm going to take what's mine, Eliza."

"Yes." Her words fanned across my mouth. "I'm yours."

My lips captured hers, claiming a small part of her for myself forever. Every kiss tasted bitterly of goodbye, of unshed tears, and nights spent in an empty bed. I shoved those thoughts aside, needing to consume myself with Eliza instead. Her delicate fingers pressed into my chest, dancing along the muscles as if committing every inch of me to memory.

There was no way I could forget anything about her—not how smooth her skin felt beneath my touch nor the way her firm, round breasts fit perfectly within my palms. As if summoned by memory, my hands set to work loosening the buttons on her blouse. The swell of her breasts peeked out over a confection of black lace. I dragged my lips along the edge, watching her chest jolt upward with each labored breath.

Both the blouse and the bra landed in a pile on the floor. I closed my mouth over one dusky nipple and circled my tongue over the taut little bud. She arched her back toward me, releasing a moan to match the one inside my head.

I could never tire of how she felt, how she made me feel every time I touched her. No other woman had ever made sex feel this good. I quickly shoved aside the voice that warned it would never feel this good again.

My hands glided along her thighs, slipping under her skirt. I gripped her tight, little ass in my hands and dragged her closer to the edge of the desk. Leaning her back, I pulled the underwear down her legs and let them join the other articles of clothing on the floor.

Her hands dove into my hair, gently tugging me back to her lips. With one long thrust, I filled her, feeling her close around my cock as if she had been made for me alone. She whimpered, and I swallowed each cry of ecstasy with a kiss. With every stroke, her body tightened around me, succumbing to a new wave of pleasure.

I watched her climax spread across her in one long, rolling

tumult of bliss, before giving in to my own. I could spend a lifetime giving her every ounce of passion she deserved—a lifetime inside a woman made only for me.

But a lifetime was no longer on the table, only five days.

So, I would have to make do with what I was given until I could convince Eliza how wrong she was.

Chapter Twenty

ELIZA

Sleeping with Justin hadn't made matters any easier.

I'd planned on telling him we should cut it short as soon as he returned to the office. There was no need to continue the extra five days, especially when there were no important events in place where our presence as a couple was necessary. We could keep our distance until Saturday, then make the announcement when ready.

Instead, he'd stepped off that elevator, and I'd practically melted all over him.

Who could blame me? The man was so fucking gorgeous, it was like sleeping with a fantasy.

In fact, it was all fantasy. There could never have been a real relationship between us, even if that's what he thought he wanted.

It was better to just leave him early and bide my time until Saturday. Make excuses for why we couldn't meet and quit my job.

Which I did and I still hated myself every second for it.

Ugh. I sound so weak right now!

No. What sounded weak was me giving in to him moments after giving myself the pep talk of a lifetime. What had he said?

You're still mine, and I'm going to take what's mine.

And I'd caved. What the hell was wrong with me?

Despite all my attempts to convince myself otherwise, I was his. Even the past three weeks without him had felt like a torture I couldn't surpass.

After hooking up with him in his office, I'd stayed late after work to clear out my desk. I'd told him a family emergency prevented me from spending the last few days with him and reiterated my desire to end things afterward.

Three weeks later, I was still technically engaged to Justin Alexander. No formal notice was ever filed. Though in three weeks, I hadn't heard so much as a word from him either. I'd tried to ignore how that made me feel. Like I was something so easily cast aside and forgotten.

He was likely just giving me the space I wanted. I was the one who had pushed for this. I was the one who had told him I didn't want to be with him, then just left like some cruel, heartless woman. Did I really expect him to fight for me? Did I expect he would come racing after me like some knight in shining armor?

You're pathetic. Truly.

"Did you tell him yet?" Gabi asked, gesturing toward the books in front of me. I had been reading the same paragraph for the past fifty minutes. It was getting me nowhere.

"No, Gabi. When would I have told him?"

"You probably should have said something to him three weeks ago," she said. "You know, when you last saw him."

"I was trying to break up with him," I explained, "not reel him back in."

"He deserves to know about the baby."

My heart sank. It was the only thing I regretted about all of this. I'd convinced myself not telling Justin was for the best. It would only hurt us both more if he knew. And yet, if he wanted to be a part of the baby's life, how would he feel if he lost out on all those moments?

I shook my head of those incessant thoughts. Family meant nothing to Justin. He made that clear on more than one occasion. Even when it came to solving his issues with his parents, he would rather throw money around to satisfy his guilt rather than face any real emotions.

No, this was all for the best.

I had come to terms with my pregnancy weeks ago. Gabi had brought me the test, and I'd cried for two hours when I learned the results. Any other person would have been overjoyed to know they were carrying the baby of the man they loved. But it was just another cruel stab of fate, twisting in the knife even deeper than before.

"Mama and Papi took the news well, I think," Gabi said, drawing me back from my thoughts.

I scoffed. "I'm still alive, aren't I?"

"Oh, come on. Mama just bought like three new sets of baby clothes, two stuffed toys, and a baby blanket." Gabi looked over her shoulder, as if conveying a grand secret. "And I think I even saw paint swatches. She was waving them around the guest room. So, thanks. There goes my bedroom."

I laughed, despite the whirl of still spinning about my head. "You don't even live here."

"I like to keep my options open." Gabi rolled a shoulder upward. "Now, the little pip-squeak has first dibs. Typical."

Silence filled in around us. I turned back to my reading material about parenting, pregnancy, and preparation for the baby's arrival. Exhaustion slowly settled in. Despite taking time off from work, I rarely slept. The morning sickness didn't help matters. I had never been so sick in my life and I'd never felt so weak, either. I could barely even eat anything. How the heck was this kid supposed to grow if I was losing weight in my first trimester?

"So?" Gabi asked.

I slammed my hand against the counter. Dammit. Between my sister and my raging thoughts, there was no way I was ever going to earn a little peace. "So what, Gabi?"

"When are you going to tell him?"

Not this again. "What good is telling him going to do? If I told Justin about the baby, he would think I tried to trap him in a marriage by getting myself pregnant."

Wasn't that the tried and true method of catching a billionaire, after all? Get yourself pregnant and either be married or set up for life. I didn't want either of those things. I didn't want a husband who resented me or a father who was no more than a paycheck to my child. I wasn't sure which would hurt more at this point. I couldn't bear the thought of him proposing out of duty alone. Yet, I couldn't handle the disgust that came with him turning away from me either.

"Things are better this way," I said, more to myself than anyone else.

"Better for you, perhaps," Gabi said. "Not better for the baby and not better for Justin. If he doesn't want to be involved, then that's up to him. If he wants to throw money at the situation, you have the option to tell him 'no'. Though why in God's name you would want to do that is beyond me."

"He already gave me more than enough money," I said. "It's enough to get Mama and Papi where they need to be. I can take time away for school and the baby. We're set. I don't need to live an extravagant life."

"You don't want to hear what he has to say." Gabi eyed me curiously. "You don't want to confirm your worst suspicions about him. That's why you haven't said anything. You're doing this to protect yourself, not the baby or Justin."

"He speaks to his family, what, twice a year?" I snapped. I could possibly blame it on the mood swings, the stress of so much change in such a short amount of time, but it would all be lies. She was right. I was terrified to learn the truth. Though I was certain I already knew it. "He didn't even go back to visit them for over ten years. He doesn't place as high a value on family as we do."

"But that's his family. It's his past he has to contend with," Gabi said. "This baby is a whole new beginning with a whole new history. There's no past attached to it beyond his feelings for you. And those were all good memories, until you freaked out and decided to run."

"I didn't freak out and run."

Gabi laughed, tossing her head back in such a flourish I almost strangled her. "*Nena*, that's what you always do. That's why you've never been in a serious relationship, why you always work part-time jobs, and why you dropped out of school."

"I dropped out of school to help our parents." Or did she already forget that part? This was insane. She was completely out of line. I didn't run from anything. I set goals. I had ambition.

Then, shouldn't I have accomplished something by now?

"That was an excuse," Gabi continued. "I could have picked up some of the extra slack, but you didn't want my help. You got scared about being done with school and of having to form a whole new plan in life. You know, be cast out into the world and see if you'd invested wisely in those four years."

Oh my God. She was right. I sabotaged myself every step of the way. Maybe I could have been happy with Justin, but I'd never allowed myself the chance. He wanted to keep things going, not as a lie, but as a legitimate relationship. I simply freaked out because of ...

The baby.

I pressed my hand against my stomach. Warmth flowed through me in a soft, kindling glow.

I was going to be a mommy.

There was a life already starting to form right there in my belly—a life bearing a little bit of me and a little bit of Justin. "What if he asks to marry me when he finds out?"

"That's a bad thing?" Gabi asked.

"I don't want him asking simply because I'm pregnant."

Gabi bobbed two hands in front of her, seemingly posing a question without asking one. "Again, this isn't really the Stone Age. So ... you don't have to get married to protect your honor. Papi isn't going to duel him or anything if that's what you're worried about."

I opened my mouth to speak but was silenced by the sound of a knock at the front door. My heart sank to the floor.

No. Dear, God. I can't do this right now.

It couldn't be Justin. It wouldn't make any sense. Why wait until now to try to contact me?

"You get the door." I shoved Gabi down the hallway.

"Really?" She cast a disappointed glare over my shoulder but moved toward the door anyway.

A sharp cramp arose in the pit of my stomach. I was going to be sick, and I hadn't even eaten anything.

"It's a woman," Gabi said, before swinging the front door open.

I recognized the woman's voice at the door before she entered the room. Kinsley looked every bit as graceful and powerful as she did the day I'd had first met her. She'd looked like a woman on a mission, ready to pluck the first candidate from the list of sacrifices. Her eyes leveled over me and then softened instantly.

"Eliza," Kinsley said sweetly while closing the distance between us. "I need you to come back to the office."

I shifted uneasily. "I thought you had already found a replacement for my position."

"Oh, we did," she said. "And then Justin promptly fired her. Along with her replacement."

I couldn't have heard that right. First, there was no way she was actually asking me to come back to work. And second, how had he already gone through two assistants in a matter of three weeks? "I don't understand."

"Turns out you were the only assistant he could tolerate." Kinsley shrugged, stating the events as if the most natural occurrence in the world. "Even more surprising is that I think he was actually *nicer* to the other assistants before you."

Just the idea of facing him so soon made my stomach turn. Not only did he revert back to his beastly behavior, but it was clear I was the catalyst behind it all. If I went back now, we would both say things we were bound to regret. Not exactly the ideal setup for springing life-altering news on him.

I shook my head, the rest of my body frozen to the floor. "Kinsley, I can't go back to work-"

"Work?" She laughed and tossed one perfectly coiffed gold ringlet over her shoulder. "Oh, honey, no. I'm not taking you back to the office to work. You need to go fix things with Justin because he is a wreck. Honestly, it's for his own safety at this point. Either you fix him, or I'm putting him out of his misery."

She leaned forward, gently squeezing my wrist as her ice blue eyes lanced through my soul. "And I don't mean that figuratively. I will literally kill him."

I pulled back. One hand flattened over my stomach. The other flew to the corner of my lip. Good Lord, this was not helping my morning sickness. "What am I supposed to do?"

"I don't know," she said. "Apologize? Make him apologize? I'm not really sure who screwed what up. But he's so damn stubborn and unreasonable right now, I thought you might be the easiest option."

Apologize? Make him apologize? The words played back in my brain like the sad little echo of a woman gone mad. My only options were to grovel at his feet, beg him for forgiveness, or exact an apology from a man too stubborn to admit he needed another human being to survive.

The churning in my belly roiled like a tempest set on pliant waters. What little food I'd eaten that morning slowly rose to my throat, and I held a hand up to excuse myself. "One second."

After five minutes of my routine torment and washing my hands and face, I peered back into the mirror. I could talk to him, but not now. I needed a day to compose my thoughts. She couldn't expect me to tame the beast in a matter of hours, could she? This sort of thing required diplomacy, strategy. It required far more time than I had.

Time. Crap! What time is it? Even if I wanted to talk with Justin, I couldn't do it today. I was forty minutes outside of a hospital appointment to complete the last bit of bloodwork and an ultrasound. I had put it all off for too long as it was and had spent the last couple of weeks pouring over baby books to ...

Shit! The baby books. My heart pounded wildly in my chest, threatening to burst through my ribcage unless thoroughly restrained. I had left all the baby books on the table, right in full view for Kinsley to find.

Maybe I would get lucky. Maybe she wouldn't notice them.

I swung the door open. Kinsley stood in the door frame, eyes latched on me like a lioness assessing a trespasser and held up one of the baby books from the table.

"What the hell is this?" she asked.

Perfect.

I exhaled and gestured toward one of the seats surrounding the small table. "You're going to need to sit down."

Chapter Twenty-One

JUSTIN

"That's all I need for now," I said and ended the call.

My fingers toyed with the square box and business card to the jeweler's before tossing them back into my coat pocket.

I could have taken the ring back at any time. Yet, for some foolish reason I'd held out hope I might still have a use for it in the future. I didn't even know why I'd bought it. I hadn't planned on proposing at the time. Though I suppose, somewhere in the back of my mind, I'd wanted it on hand just in case.

Three weeks without Eliza, and I had the answer I'd so desperately tried to avoid.

I needed her.

Three weeks without her may as well have been three years. And yet, for all the pain it caused, it felt like mere moments since she'd walked out my door. If I'd known that day in my office would have been our last, I might have been better prepared to fight for her. But now, with so many days between us, I didn't even know where to start.

Without so much as a word from her, it became increasingly clear Eliza did not feel the same way about me. I'd tried to give her space, to let her arrive at whatever conclusion she needed to make up her mind.

What else was a man like me to do, after all? Begging seemed beneath a person in my position. If I wasn't what she wanted, then it was a reality I had to face sooner or later. So, I'd told myself to muscle through the pain like a good soldier and convinced myself that a wounded pride had nothing to do with the fact that I hadn't contacted her myself.

In fact, that was just what I needed. I could handle her telling me she didn't love me. Right now, I needed to hear it much more than the silence. At least that way I could move on with my life and find another way to handle all this pent-up frustration.

God, I'm an asshole.

I sifted through the blurred haze of events over the past few weeks. I was back to a revolving door of assistants, with Kinsley setting up a new interview each week. I'd already gone through two perfectly capable assistants in a span of only two weeks. That's right. I could even admit they were capable. There was absolutely nothing wrong with the women Kinsley sent me.

They just weren't Eliza.

My phone lit up with a photo of my parents and my mother's name listed below. I answered it. "Yes, Mother?"

"I hear congratulations are in order." Her voice filtered in through the receiver like music.

"More congratulations?" My body tensed in anticipation. The

last time she congratulated me on anything, I wound up engaged to my assistant.

"Yes. You finally landed the Montgomery Plantation."

I sighed, pushing down the flood of unease settling in, in its place. I had only received confirmation from Rosalie this morning, which didn't even seem enough time to tell Kinsley. "How in the hell does news travel so fast in that town?"

"We probably heard about it long before you did," she explained. "Rosalie asked a few people around town to help her make her decision. Sawyer sure wasn't too happy about the conclusion, but he already seems to be over it and on to the next order of business."

A soft chuckle erupted in the base of my throat. "Imagine that."

"So, does this mean you'll be coming back soon?" The note of hope in her voice caused the slowly forming knot in my chest to tighten. "Everyone keeps asking if you'll be moving back home. I told them, with Eliza's parents, it wasn't likely to be any time soon."

Fuck. How much longer could I keep this going? I'd let the engagement stand, still waiting to hear back from Rosalie before making anything official. When it came to this point in the game, I'd never imagined how I would feel. All the disappointment I'd attempted to avoid rushed toward me in full force, more powerful than if I'd simply set the record straight from the beginning.

And why? Because now, my family wasn't the only one disappointed, and the only thing standing between me and my happiness was my damned pride.

"I'll be back next week," I said finally.

"That's wonderful. For how long?"

The way her mood shifted suggested she had something specific planned. "Do you have a time frame in mind, Mother?"

"Well, we are heading into Christmas territory. It would be nice to have you home for the holidays for once."

God, dammit. I'm a fucking mess. I'd buried myself so deeply in my work trying to avoid my feelings, I'd nearly forgotten about the holiday all together. Thank God Kinsley was in charge of all the bonuses and parties, otherwise I'd be losing far more staff than just two assistants.

I dragged my thoughts back to the question at hand. Could I really handle Christmas at home? I'd spent so many years running from ghosts, I had neglected the parts of my life that made me feel alive—family, friendship, love. I'd pushed everyone away, people who did nothing but remind me of a guilt I could barely withstand. Kinsley was the only real friend I had left, and I treated her more like an assistant than a confidant.

And Eliza ...

My fingertips pressed against my temples, alleviating the building tension. I hadn't even tried to make things work between us. I'd simply let her go.

I was a damn fool.

"I'll stay the week." The words sounded foreign on my lips.

"Splendid. Of course, the invitation extends to Eliza, as well," she said. "If her father is well enough to travel, her family is more than welcome to join us. Most of the bed and breakfast is rented out at this time of year, but we do have a couple of rooms left. I'm sure we can find a way to accommodate everyone."

I can't do this anymore. I ran a hand along my face, clearing away the last lingering doubts that convinced me keeping up this charade did less damage than the truth. "I think it's time I ..."

"We need to talk." The door to my office swung open. Kinsley stood in the doorway. She panted heavily, as if she'd raced up the stairs rather than taken the elevator.

"Mother, I'll call you back," I said, then hung up the phone without awaiting an answer. "What is it? What's wrong?"

Kinsley shifted nervously. Her eyes tilted upward, attempting to draw whatever inspiration the ceiling offered to form her words. "Eliza is in the hospital."

By the time I'd managed forty minutes of rush hour traffic and three sets of medical staff, I had finally found the right person to point me in Eliza's direction. The rush of blood in my ears echoed a fatal warning that any more stress might send the rest of my body into shock. The soldier in me used all ties to adrenaline to forge ahead, maintain focus, and utilize this outburst of energy toward something productive.

So, when I found her in the hallway, completely whole and seemingly unscathed, I released a much-needed sigh of relief and fought down any urge to press her back against the wall and make love to her right there.

"Eliza." Her name escaped my lips in a strangled plea. I sounded whipped as hell but was too worried to care.

She jolted, freezing instantly as recognition settled in. "Justin?"

"Are you alright?" I reached for her.

To my surprise, she didn't pull away. Instead, her body curled into my embrace, tugging me tighter and rekindling desires I convinced myself I could live without. Now, after all that time, no doubts remained.

Eliza Cortez was mine, and I would spend a lifetime convincing her no one else would ever do.

"Yes, I'm fine." She nodded and tucked her chin against my chest. "What are you doing here?"

"What am I doing here?" I tugged her back, forcing her to hold my gaze. "Kinsley said you were in the hospital."

Eliza rolled her eyes and whispered a curse under her breath. "I'm fine. Kinsley just has a sick sense of humor."

"Sense of humor?" The adrenaline in my veins gradually gave way to anger. Not only had Kinsley manipulated me, Eliza thought nothing of her current status in the hospital. "What's going on?"

She pulled away, taking my hand in hers and drawing me into one of the empty rooms. Eliza's gaze shifted anxiously from the door to her feet. She chewed her lower lip as she dove a hand into her purse and removed a thin sheet of paper. She swallowed hard as I clenched it between my fingertips.

A black and white photo depicted an amorphous blob that looked like it had been ripped from the pages of a sci-fi novel. It took a moment for the image to sink in. When it did, that same flood of panic and excitement welled within me.

"Is that ...?" The words caught in my throat.

Her jaw tensed. She choked down another swallow before nodding stiffly.

I peered back down at the image in front of me. Only this time, a sudden sense of pride overtook me, one set against an odd feeling of hopefulness. "I'm going to be a dad?"

Her chest rose abruptly. The slightest tremor rippled through her lip, as if she might burst into tears at any moment. Though she quickly clamped it down. "Yes."

I took a step forward. "Why didn't you say anything?"

"I don't know." She shrugged and took an uneasy step back. "I mean, I could give you a list of reasons. I didn't want you to feel responsible for something I was perfectly capable of handling on my own."

I bit down the fury building at her words. Did she have any intention of telling me at all? If Kinsley hadn't forced me to come down here, would I have carried on my whole life without ever knowing my child?

"Eliza, this isn't like you were asking me to wash the dishes." A low growl pulsed through my words. "This is a child."

"What does that matter to you?" she asked, as unnerved by my tone as I was hearing her confession. "When has family, or being there for people who care about you, ever mattered?"

Now, it made sense. This was still somehow my fault—my past coming back to haunt me. But I was not alone in letting my feelings of guilt and fear overpower me. Eliza could not lay all the blame at my feet, not for this.

"This is why you left?" I asked, fighting back the scoff that emerged to no avail. "You assumed I would just abandon you, so you thought you would cut me to the chase."

"I didn't want you to feel obligated to say things you didn't really feel."

A pang of ice stabbed through the center of my chest. The chill froze me down to the core, spreading throughout my body like the cold grip of death. We had been playing this game for so long, we'd forgotten to establish what was real. I'd never actually told Eliza how I felt about her. I'd never told her this was no longer a game of appearances and deception.

It hadn't been for quite some time.

I had just assumed she knew how I felt—that every time I'd held her and kissed her, it spoke volumes to how desperately I'd fallen in love with her.

Except it hadn't.

Instead, when she'd needed confirmation most, I'd told her we should set a time limit on our relationship. When she had pushed me away and said she'd wanted something real, I didn't even tell her that it already was.

I had just let her go.

I wouldn't make that same mistake twice.

"And what words would I be obligated to say?" I asked, closing the remaining distance between us in two small strides.

Her eyes flicked upward, holding mine with a molten glare. My hand closed about her waist. Every inch of my body reacted to her, feeling her warmth and the underlying fire, like a salve to an old wound.

"I need you?" I asked, pressing a kiss against her temple. She tensed beneath my hands. "I love you? Marry me?"

"Stop." She pushed back.

I tightened my grip, holding her firmly against me. My head dipped down to her ear, and she shivered as my words feathered across her cheek. "Why? Because you don't want to hear it? Or you don't know how to respond?"

"Because I want it to be real and not something I coerced out of you."

My hand glided up her back, tangling my fingers in her hair. There was no way I was ever going to let this woman out of my life again, no way I would ever let her doubt my feelings for her or how badly I needed her by my side.

"Despite what you might think, I am a grown man, Eliza. I don't need anyone to tell me what decisions to make." I tugged gently on the strands of hair within my grasp, tilting her head back to peer up into my gaze. Her golden eyes poured into me like streams of sunshine. Every ounce of longing I had suffered in the last three weeks without her begged me to take her in that moment. "I just *want* to make those decisions *with you*."

I kissed her, reclaiming every minute of time lost to pride and my carelessness. Her body relaxed against me. Whatever doubts she'd harbored faded away until nothing remained beyond a primal desire locked away for far too long. My tongue slid past the seam of her lips, conquering yet another part of her soul she kept locked away. With every kiss and every touch, she surrendered to the possibilities, and I fell even further than before.

When I pulled away, she stared back at me, dazed and breathless.

"I'll take you home," I said and took her by the hand. "I need to discuss a few things with your family."

"Like what?" she asked. All the anger and stubbornness from before dissolved, unearthing the woman I spent weeks drawing out of her stone fortress.

"Christmas. Among other things."

She eyed me carefully, following me down the hall toward the hospital exit. "What do you mean 'Christmas'? I thought you usually spent it working or home alone."

"Yes, well, my mother expects me home this Christmas," I explained. "And I am happy to oblige her."

"You're going home?" Disbelief colored her every word. "For Christmas?"

I laughed lightly, amused by the look of shock on her face. "That surprises you?"

"Obviously. But then ..."

Then, where did that leave us? I didn't want to spend the holiday away from Eliza either—especially now. Though I could respect her wanting to stay home with her own family rather than dragging them all the way across the other side of the country.

"You are welcome to join me, you and your family," I said. Even if she said no, we would make it work the same way every other couple did around this time of year. "My mother said they have enough room for everyone. But if that's too much, or if you're not ready, I can work out another arrangement. We can—"

"No, I ..." She held a hand up to silence me, stopping just outside the hospital entrance. Her arms wrapped about her. "That's fine. I'm just trying to process all of this."

I paced myself with one long, wavering breath. My eyes slid down to her stomach. "I know what you mean."

The news hadn't quite sunk in all the way yet. Twenty minutes ago, I had thought Eliza to be on her deathbed, alone and slowly fading away in a cold hospital bed. Hell, an hour ago, I thought we might never even see each other again.

And now? I was back to visions of white picket fences and a life with a woman who drove me completely insane—only add a smaller, much more chaotic, version of the woman I loved to the mix.

If I knew nothing about being a husband, I sure as hell knew even less about being a dad. But heaven help me, I wanted to learn.

"I don't even know where to begin," I said, more to myself than anyone else.

Eliza smiled and all doubts melted away like the last remnants of snow in soft spring rain. "Names? Nursery themes?"

I let her smile lure me away from the dark, persistent thoughts in the back of my mind. The ones full of "what-ifs" and too many questions to keep sane. One stood out among all the others.

Her hand grazed my arm, drawing me back to her. Those same warm, honey-colored eyes seemed to know exactly where I went and what I needed to hear.

"I would have told you," she said, softly, "eventually."

"Would you?"

She withdrew her touch, and I felt the loss of it instantly. "I didn't want to at first. Even after I'd talked to Kinsley, I had thought maybe ... it was best for everyone. Then during the ultrasound, I saw the baby, and all I could think about was how much love I already had for someone I hadn't even met yet. And then ..."

Her voice trailed off. Something caught in her throat, but she quickly choked it down. "And then, all I wanted was you. I can face whatever challenges are ahead, but I would rather face them together."

I leaned down and pressed a soft kiss to her lips. "Seems we're finally on the same page for once."

A gentle tremor pulsed through her as I pulled away. The light misting of rain brought a new chill to the air, and I draped my coat over her shoulders. I spent no longer than a minute exchanging information with the valet to bring my car back around. When I faced her, she had slid her arms through the coat sleeves and held the small black jewelry box between her fingers.

"Justin?" Her words quivered with suspicion more than shock. "What is this?"

The words stuck in my throat. Every inch of me froze, and my feet fused to the ground. There was a long story attached to that box. It was one that required more than a brief conversation on the curb of a hospital.

"It ..." *What the hell do I even say?* I couldn't propose to her there in the most unromantic location I could imagine—not while we were still nursing a month's worth of wounds. "This isn't exactly how I'd imagined it playing out in my head."

She held the business card I stuffed into my coat along with it out to me, as if evidence of some unknown deceit. "You bought this in New York?"

I nodded.

"That's over three weeks ago," she said.

"I'm well aware."

"So, was this just another prop? Or ..." Her voice cracked and she lowered her head toward the objects in her hands. Every breath sent her chest soaring upward in ragged, little gasps. I plucked the box from between her fingers and examined the ring as if truly seeing it for the first time.

"I had every intention of coming home and leaving our engagement as it was," I said. "Until I was ready to use this."

She swallowed a sharp gulp of air, calming her nerves to steady her thoughts. "You wanted to marry me?"

"No." I shook my head. My fingers gripped her chin and

tipped her gaze upward to meet mine. "I'm *going* to marry you. You can't keep running from me."

The corner of her lip lifted in shaken amusement. She tilted one pointed brow upward. "Is that an order?"

"It's a request," I said. "From a man who loves you more than life itself."

My lips brushed lightly against hers, whispering promises and assurances words could not express. Her body molded into mine. Every breath, every touch spoke of home, and I knew there would never be another woman for me—only Eliza.

"Well?" I asked. "Are you ready to make an honest man out of me?"

She bit her lip, holding back the slightest tilt of a smile. "Yes."

A rush of warmth flowed across my chest, slow and melting like sweet, summer honey. I slid the ring onto her finger and kissed her once again, claiming her mouth, her body, and soul as mine alone.

When I pulled away, her words tumbled out in a breathless sigh. "I love you."

"I love you, Eliza, always." I smiled and brought her fingers to my lips. "Now, let's go home."

EPILOGUE

wo Years Later

"It's beautiful," I said, peering up at the stacks of hay and pumpkins lining the edges of the white veranda.

Shimmering lanterns trailed down the cobblestone path, creating a warm, orange haze perfect for a crisp autumn evening. "It's just like I remember."

"Some slight adjustments," Justin said. "Though I'll admit. Rosalie does know how to throw a party."

Two years ago, we had walked down this very driveway to join Rosalie for her annual fall celebration. It was the one stipulation she'd requested in the property deal—one night to host the masquerade gala she claimed was nearly a century's worth of tradition in the making.

And how could we refuse? Not only was the event the perfect place to network and regroup with those invested in

Justin's charity, but it also had quickly transformed into a marvelous opportunity to raise funds for the coming year.

Rosalie greeted us at the front, ever the gracious hostess and looking as radiant as ever.

"You two look amazing," she said, pressing a kiss against my cheek. "How's the little one? I can't wait to see her tomorrow."

"She's with my parents," Justin explained, sliding a brief look in my direction. "Wreaking havoc no doubt. She's quite stubborn for a one year old. I wonder where she gets it."

I raised a brow upward, pinning him with as cool a stare as I could muster. It was a mythical feat to accomplish really. Whenever he looked at me with that roguish, dashing smile, my knees seemed to melt out from beneath me.

"Really? This is all my fault?" I asked. "It has absolutely nothing to do with the fact that she has her father already wrapped around her finger?"

Justin opened his mouth to speak, arriving at no other conclusion than silence. He clenched his jaw shut, admittedly defeated. A sheepish grin slipped across his face, and he leaned toward Rosalie. "It was nice seeing you again."

She flashed a knowing smile as we disappeared into the ballroom.

"Wrapped around her finger, huh?" Justin asked, pulling me to a quiet corner of the room. I peered up at him, unable to hide my amusement. His hands wrapped around my waist, squeezing gently as he brought me flush against him. "Like mother, like daughter."

He bent his head down to mine, capturing my lips in a kiss that demanded as much pleasure as it gave. Heat curled deep within my belly. It enlivened a familiar, sweet ache that pulsed down between my thighs. When he pulled away, his voice grumbled low and deep. "Eliza, I need you, now."

"Right now?" My eyes shifted to the surrounding area. There was hardly anyone close enough to hear us, though it would still be difficult to sneak away unnoticed. "You can't wait?"

Another grumble erupted in the base of his throat. "It's tradition. I have to have my way with you at least once on the grounds before we leave."

Desire set my skin aflame, shooting molten currents of electricity to every corner of my body. "Two times doesn't make it a tradition."

"Then three will." His lips trailed down my throat. A new string of sensations webbed its way down to my toes. Good God, this man was dangerous. "Besides, I know where all the secret passageways are."

The pressure inside me continued to build. *For heaven's sake! He's barely even touched me yet.* I was near shaking by the time I nodded, only able to exhale one word in response. "Yes."

Without a moment to hesitate, he dragged me across the room and toward one of the hidden doorways leading to the old slave quarters. We disappeared into a small, dimly lit tunnel, stopping halfway as he pressed me back against the wall. Our bodies merged in a tangle of lips and limbs, unable to control our desire any longer.

"I hope you know what you're doing," I said, surprised by how winded my words sounded. "If we get caught—"

"They'll what?" he asked, gently tugging the sleeves of my dress down my shoulder. "Kick me out of my own property?"

He took one nipple between his teeth, teasing the tight bud with a flick of his tongue. The sheer heat of his mouth closing over me trembled through me in soft shudders of ecstasy. "It'll probably end up in the papers."

"You think so?" His hands bunched around my dress, lifting the edges until they clung up above my waist. "What would the headline read anyway? 'Billionaire Makes Love to His Gorgeous Wife'? Not much of a scandal if you ask me."

His fingers found my core, dancing along the slick folds in a rhythm only he knew. My hips bucked against his touch, wanting more of him, wanting all of him.

"I'm intrigued," I replied, biting my lip and suppressing a moan as his hands continued their wicked devotion.

"I bet you are." He leaned against me, pressing a kiss to my temple before filling me completely with his hard length. My body constricted around him, full and whole for the first time in what felt like an eternity.

I could never get enough of him. Not after two years and not ever in a lifetime.

He was mine, wholly and completely.

And in his embrace, I would forever feel at home.

GET YOUR FREE BOOK

Have you read the FREE Prequel to Beauty and the BOSS?

If not, sign up for my Newsletter and download your FREE book.

Click this Link to Download your FREE book

Beauty and the BOSS is the first book in the Billionaire's Obsession Series and is available here -> Read Beauty and the BOSS

Lawyer and the BOSS is the 2nd book in the Billionaire's Obsession Series and is available here -> Read Lawyer and the BOSS

Nanny and the BOSS is the 3rd book in the Billionaire's Obsession Series and is available here -> Read Nanny and the BOSS

Teacher and the BOSS is the 4th book in the Billionaire's Obsession Series and is available here -> Read Teacher and the BOSS

Innkeeper and the BOSS is the 5th and final book in the Billionaire's Obsession Series and is available here -> Read Innkeeper and the BOSS

SNEEK PEAK INTO FORBIDDEN DOCTOR

Forbidden Doctor is Book 4 in the "Forbidden Fairy Tales" series and is the story of **Stevie and Adrian.**

Each book in this series is a Standalone and can be read in any order.

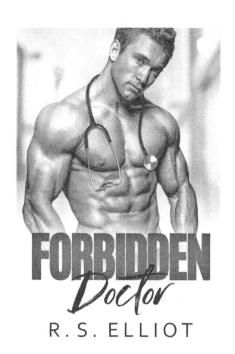

Click this link to READ Forbidden Doctor!!

ADRIAN

*T*here were very few times in my life that I was at a loss for words.

Sitting between Jonah and Louise, with only my best friend as a barrier between myself and the girl I'd slept with, I was finding it hard to think of anything to say.

It didn't help that Jonah almost immediately offered to switch places.

"She wants to go into cardiothoracics, Ade! If there's anyone at this table she needs to talk to, it's definitely you!"

So then, I was placed next to her. She was determinedly looking down at her plate, where a hardboiled egg and some salad sat. If I didn't know what was happening, I'd have thought the food had some mesmerizing property. Trying to collect my thoughts into something coherent, I looked up, only to be met with the stern gaze of Dr. Aaron Christophers.

Fuck.

When I had been told we'd be meeting his daughter, and I'd met the girl at Sweet Nell's that spoke about him with bitterness in her voice, I hadn't made the connection. For someone supposedly so smart, I was freaking dumb. Everyone at the table thought he was just about the best Chief of Surgery you could ask for, and while he was efficient at his job, I also knew how ruthless he could be.

So not only had I screwed one of the new residents, I had managed to screw the chief's daughter. I wanted to crawl into a hole for a few days while I figured everything out.

"So, um, Stephanie," I said, turning to face her and wrenching my gaze from Aaron's. "You're interested in cardio-thoracics?"

Clearly bracing herself, the girl I now knew was named Stephanie looked up at me and nodded. I should have braced myself as well.

She was just as stunning as the night before. Sure, she looked tired and nervous, but everything else about her was beautiful—something I hadn't expected when the alcohol wore off. She was wearing a long, floral dress that buttoned up the front. It was beautiful on her—but didn't suit the fiery girl I'd met last night.

It made her look more like the embodiment of spring, her chocolate-honey hair pulled into a ponytail and a few flyaway strands framing her face. Her eyes didn't meet mine directly; she appeared to be making contact with a point somewhere just above my eyes. I was pretty sure she had makeup on, but it didn't mask her natural beauty, only accented it. Her freckles made her look younger than she was, especially paired with the dress, but the dark warning I caught in her eyes suggested exactly the opposite.

We could never be together.

We could never sleep together again. What we needed was to move on, but it wouldn't be possible with the proximity in which we'd be working, especially if she was planning to head into my area of expertise. It would be a cruel and unusual punishment to force her out of cardiothoracics simply for the sake of a job I had already secured. I was in a position of power, and her face said she knew that.

There was more to her though, more than a great night. I couldn't shake the idea that she was someone I was supposed to know. We couldn't be together, but that didn't mean we couldn't be friends. I was curious what secrets those hazel eyes held, what richness they could grant to my life. It had been a while since someone had been so interesting that I knew I had to be connected to them, but then Stephanie Christophers apparently could change that.

"Well, it will be great to have you on the team," I said with as much cheeriness as I could muster. "We're always looking for new talent."

"Thanks," Stephanie said quietly.

I poured myself some coffee and hoped that the caffeine would be enough to stop me from embarrassing myself.

"So, are you going to put her through her paces, Ade?" Angela asked from across the table.

I rolled my eyes.

"Yeah, Angela, because hazing is both humane and legal."

"Probably was when you were a resident, old man," Jonah laughed, nudging me.

"I'm only four years older than you!"

"And in four years, I, too, will be an old man," he cackled.

Stephanie watched the whole exchange with wide eyes.

"Wait, so that makes you..." she said slowly.

"Thirty-five," I stated.

Oh crap. I knew I looked younger than my age, but was she finding it creepy that I had gone home with her? I already knew that she was some kind of genius, having graduated two years earlier than most. That would make her twenty-four.

So, she had slept with a man eleven years her senior and was probably regretting it. Those eyes were unreadable though. I had a feeling they'd be unreadable even if she made direct eye contact with me. I couldn't tell what she was thinking, but I could guess it was nothing good.

I was only at the brunch for a grand total of forty minutes. I found myself in my car again, with Angela in the front seat and Jonah relegated to the back for being a loudmouth. I had offered to drive them back to the hospital, but my thoughts were anywhere but at my workplace.

The short ride seemed faster than usual, and without registering parking or saying goodbye to my coworkers, I was in my office. There was a pile of papers on the desk, things that needed sorting, things that needed approval. I sat for only a moment, before putting down my current project and standing. It was all wordy jargon. With as calm a mannerism as I could manage, I strode over to the blinds that let me look out onto the ward and pulled the string. One of the nurses gave me a strange look, but I just smiled at her. They probably assumed I was going to change.

Instead, I did something I hadn't done since my senior year

of high school. I pulled the sofa from the wall and lined it up with the empty side of my desk, with only enough space for me to fit between them. I sat in the middle of the sofa, placed my forehead on the edge of the desk, and stared at the floor.

I was sure I'd look strange to anyone that happened to walk in, but the perks of having your own office meant people had to knock first. When my mother passed away, I had done this every morning. It had helped me center myself before dealing with school. I had spent ten minutes feeling everything that my mind and body needed me to feel, and then I would get back up and continue on with my life. As ridiculous as it sounded, it had kept me sane.

Now though, I felt like it had the opportunity to only make things worse. Instead of confusion and fear washing over me like I had expected, memories from the night before came in spades. Stephanie spread out below me, her curls a halo, her mouth open in a small "O". I felt myself driving into her warmth, again and again, as her eyes rolled back in her head and her thighs began to quiver. I had never seen a more beautiful sight than her last night, and definitely hadn't expected to find that kind of beauty in a stranger.

I couldn't deny that part of me that also remembered how fucking *hot* she looked. I felt my blood run south, and my unruly mind instead imagined her bent over the very desk my head was resting on, spread out on the sofa where I was sat. I imagined taking her apart a hundred different ways. I'd make her scream and cover her mouth so only I could hear.

FORBIDDEN
Doctor

R.S. ELLIOT

Click this Link to Continue Reading Stevie and Adrian's story!!

Made in the USA
Middletown, DE
27 December 2022

20559958R00139